LUCIFER'S HOLD

When Elizabeth Allwood's mother dies, her last words to her eldest daughter are, 'Look after Merry.' However, Elizabeth finds it hard to cope with her spoilt sister, especially when Merry meets magician Lucas Silver. Elizabeth dislikes Lucas on sight and is fearful of his supernatural powers. When Merry's son is born, Elizabeth is determined that Lucas will not dominate him, as he does her sister. But Silver's power is great and finally Elizabeth must throw herself on the mercy of the man she hates.

Books by Sara Judge
in the Linford Romance Library:

THE GYPSY'S RETURN

SARA JUDGE

LUCIFER'S HOLD

Complete and Unabridged

LINFORD
Leicester

First published in Great Britain in 1983 by
Robert Hale Limited

First Linford Edition
published 2004
by arrangement with
Robert Hale Limited
London

British Library CIP Data

Judge, Sara
    Lucifer's hold.—Large print ed.—
    Linford romance library
    1. Love stories
    2. Large type books
    I. Title
    823.9'14 [F]

    ISBN 1–84395–325–0

Published by
F. A. Thorpe (Publishing)
Anstey, Leicestershire

Set by Words & Graphics Ltd.
Anstey, Leicestershire
Printed and bound in Great Britain by
T. J. International Ltd., Padstow, Cornwall

This book is printed on acid-free paper

To Margie

1

This is the story of my sister, Meredith Jane Allwood, who was born on the sixteenth day of June, in the year 1861.

Merry was everything that I was not; she was small-boned and blue-eyed, with golden hair and an elfin face. She was like her name, bubbling over with high spirits and ceaseless chatter. Yet when our mother died, her last words to me were 'Elizabeth, look after Merry'.

Although Merry was an enchanting little girl, she was also frivolous and rather selfish, and Mother's words to me were not always easy to obey. Father did not help me, either. He was ill, poor man, during his last years, having never recovered from Mother's death, but he spoilt Merry and would not often allow me to reprove her.

My sister brightened our lives, it is

true, but I did not always feel like laughing with Father being ill, and lack of money, and the constant caring for the sick man as well as all the housework and cooking to do.

Father received a small pension from the bank where he had worked, but I realised that we would have to go carefully, for Merry loved pretty clothes and Father needed an increasing number of pills and medicines, which Dr Poole ordered for him. Yet when I suggested that Merry should seek employment when she left school, Father was angry and Merry tearful.

'Never shall I allow a daughter of mine to go out to work,' said Father huffily, staring at me with his faded blue eyes which had once been the same colour as Merry's.

We had both been educated at Miss Bloster's establishment in the town; our schooling had eaten up most of Father's savings, but he had deemed it worthwhile. He could not abide ignorance, and although Mother had been lowly born, he had taught her to read and write, and theirs had been a truly happy marriage.

'How can you suggest such a thing?' Merry pouted. 'Mother always said I would make a good marriage, and that is what I intend to do. You go out to work, Elizabeth, if extra money is so important to you. You are built for physical labour and do not care about your appearance.'

I was the strong one, big, like my mother, with brown eyes and thick dark hair, and it was to me that Father called when his back ached, and to whom Merry ran with her headaches and little worries and woes. I was no white-fingered lady and would gladly have laboured for my family's benefit, but one had to remain practical, and it would not have made sense to leave the house, and my ailing father, in Merry's dainty hands.

Fortunately we possessed a good friend in Miss Bloster, who owned the School for Young Ladies in town, and she suggested that my sister would make an acceptable companion to an elderly lady of her acquaintance.

'Mrs Drew is a widow, with one grown son,' she said, 'and as her sight is failing and her health none too good, she is seeking a young and energetic companion, who will stay with her whilst her son is at work, and who will read to her and converse in an agreeable manner. Meredith would be well-suited to such employment, and as Mrs Drew is a lady of moderate means she will be able to pay your sister a small salary, which will doubtless help you all, Elizabeth.'

Merry decided that she liked the idea, and after meeting Mrs Drew and finding out the details of her far from arduous work, announced that the position was to her liking, and that she would begin in the Drew household on the following Monday. Father could not disagree with Miss Bloster, who had been one of Mother's few friends, and after seeing that Merry no longer objected to such occupation, he gave his reluctant consent.

Merry was sixteen years old when she entered the Drew household, and for a year all went well and she carried out her duties faithfully and happily. Father and I did not benefit financially, however, as my sister delighted in having money to spend on herself. And how could I blame her? She earned the money and therefore had the right to spend it as she wished. But as she spent every day with Mrs Drew except for Sundays, and was given a mid-day meal as well as a light supper before coming home, her absence at meal times helped my household expenses. I saw that Father continued to receive nourishing meals, whilst bread and cheese sufficed for me.

Merry's work with Mrs Drew introduced a new person into our lives that winter of 1877. Young Mr Arthur Drew began walking my sister home during the dark evenings, and he used to stay on and have a chat to Father before he left. He worked as a clerk in the same bank where Father had been employed, and I was grateful when the younger man talked to Father and brought him up to date with business news.

We seldom had visitors, for our parents had been totally content in their own company, and Mother had been an aloof, silent woman, not given to gossiping, or casual friendships. I never knew any of my grandparents, and Mother informed me once, when I was old enough to begin questioning, that she and Father had married against his family's wishes.

'My parents are both dead and I was an only child,' she told me, 'but your father's family would have nothing more to do with him after our wedding.' Her face broke into one of its rare smiles. 'They felt that he was marrying beneath him, and no doubt a farm labourer's daughter was a poor match in the eyes of Edward Allwood's family. But we have had more than our fair share of happiness, Elizabeth, and I hope that both my daughters will be blessed with as fine a man as their father.'

Theirs was a good marriage, and memories of my childhood are filled with contentment; but then Mother died and Father became ill, and life was not so cheerful. However, Mr Arthur Drew helped us in his quiet, gentle way, and I hoped that he might propose to Merry.

He was a tall man with a pale complexion, and a soft drooping moustache. His eyes reminded me of a spaniel's, and I felt that he would be good for Merry; she was so flighty and high-spirited, it would benefit her to have the company of a more serious nature.

But such a union was not to be, for the following June a letter arrived for Father.

A letter was such an extraordinary occurrence in our household that I stayed with Father whilst he opened it. We had never received any post, for with no relations and but a few friends in the neighbourhood, who would write to us?

'It is from Cousin Grace,' said Father, in such a strange voice that I pulled up a chair beside his bed and leaned forward.

'Who is Cousin Grace and what does she want?'

'She wants you or Merry,' he answered, and lay back against the pillows allowing the pages to drop on to the coverlet.

Hastily I picked up the papers.

'My dear Edward,' I read. 'It is a very long time since we have communicated with each other, but I hope that any harsh words said in the past will long since have been forgotten. Now that you are also without your loved one, perhaps you will think more kindly of me. For I have recently lost my dearest Cedric and unlike you, have no children to comfort me.

'I beg you, dear Edward, to allow one of your girls to visit me here in London.

I have been left well provided for — but what is wealth if one is lonely? I would be forever grateful if you could spare me a daughter, and I assure you that I shall look upon her as my own. Yours in hope, Grace.'

'Who is this cousin?' I asked in astonishment. 'And why have we heard nothing of her before?'

'She is my last remaining relative and her mother and mine were sisters and lived in the same part of Hampshire. But then Grace married, a man by many years her senior, and vastly wealthy, and her new station in life went to my cousin's head.' Father sighed and I thought that he looked very tired. 'She could never forgive me for marrying your dear mother. I was working in the bank here in Sussex by then, and once I saw your mother no other woman was good enough for me. You know what I felt for her, Elizabeth.' He patted my hand. 'But she was of humble stock, had neither name nor possessions, and Grace would not accept her.'

'And now she is punished for her stupidity by loneliness. How could anyone not like Mother?' I cried indignantly.

'They never met, for Grace would not come here and we received no invitation to London. But we did not need her approval, Elizabeth, we had a good life all together, did we not?'

'Indeed we did.' I stood up briskly as Father's eyes began to water. 'Now, this is the very thing for Merry. No doubt Cousin Grace wants to make amends, so it will suit both sides of the family. It should prove more interesting than looking after poor blind Mrs Drew.'

Father blinked and tried to smile. 'How do you know that Cousin Grace is not also going blind? Or bed-ridden like me? Oh, child, I had thought perhaps that you would go and I could not have borne that.'

'Me? How could I leave you?' I collected up the sheets of the letter. 'This is just capital, Father, the very thing for my sister. And if Cousin Grace has money then even if she is troubled by bad health, there must be servants in plenty to aid her.'

'Elizabeth,' said Father quietly, 'sit down. You are always rushing about, working too hard, I worry about you. Tell me truthfully, would you not like to take up this offer? Go to London and lead a gay life?'

I stared down at him. 'You cannot mean that?'

'I do, my dear, and want you to consider the idea most carefully; for I am selfish and difficult and would keep you with me always — you remind me so of your sweet mother. But this is a golden opportunity, and being the eldest you must have the right to decide.'

'And what would become of you?'

'I expect we could come to some arrangement with Mrs Stubbs, and I do not believe that it would be for long; my days are numbered, Elizabeth.'

'Don't say that!' I sank down on the

chair again and put my arms around his frail body. 'You will live for years and years, Father, and of course I should not dream of leaving you. Merry is the one who should go, she will love all the glitter and excitement of London whilst you know it would not suit me. And Mrs Stubbs may do very well for a couple of hours when we need her, but I should never allow her to take over the house. How can you think such a thing!' And I gave him a little shake.

Merry was delighted with the scheme, and spent every last penny of her wages on new gowns and bonnets.

'I cannot arrive looking like a frump, Elizabeth, and have the servants laughing behind my back. Cousin Grace will have lots of servants, won't she?'

'I presume so. Father says that her husband was a wealthy man so I have no doubt that our cousin lives in style.'

'Good, for I do not intend running around for her as I have done this last year for Mrs Drew. I want to live like a lady, Elizabeth, and have handsome gentlemen calling at the house to see me, and I want to dance and wear beautiful jewels and live a life of luxury.'

'I am sure you will.' I smiled at my sister's excited face. 'But money is not the most important thing in life, Merry.'

'Good health and happiness,' mimicked my sister, 'dear Elizabeth, you have your Miss Bloster face on again — so prim and proper — it does not become you. Don't you see — ' she twirled, clapping her hands, 'if I have money I shall *be* happy! And if one is ill, money helps, too. Look how worried you are about Father, and all those doctor's bills. If we had plenty of money you would not be anxious, *and* we could afford more servants than Mrs Stubbs once a week, and you would not have to work so hard.'

'True.' I could not contradict her. 'We shall miss you, Merry, so write often, please, and do not forget Father. He will want news of you, it will lighten his long days.'

'I shall write and make you quite

envious!' Then she sobered and caught hold of my hand. 'But you must visit, Elizabeth. Once I am settled you must come to London and see how I am getting on. It is not fair that you should be always working like a drudge whilst I am enjoying myself.'

She was kind, my sister, when she remembered, and her words warmed me. 'I do not see how I can leave Father, but your letters will do very well. And Mr Arthur will be wanting news of you, also. Poor man, I think he will miss you as much as we shall.'

'Mr Arthur Drew — pooh!' Merry tossed her head, making the ringlets bounce on her shoulders. 'I am going to meet sophisticated gentlemen who will escort me to the opera, and dance divinely. Mr Arthur is only interested in his books and his old mother. He is pleasant enough, but such a *bore*, Elizabeth!'

Before I could reprimand her she was at my side, her hand patting my brow.

'Do not frown, it is ageing. And

Elizabeth, please may I borrow your pearls? I cannot arrive at Cousin Grace's without a jewel to my name, and I'll return them the moment she gives me some of my own.'

The pearls were my most treasured possession, given to our mother by Father on their tenth wedding anniversary. He had wanted me to have them when she died, and although I never had occasion to wear them, I would take them out of their velvet-lined box whenever I was weary or depressed, and their smooth, soft beauty always calmed me.

'You will take the greatest care of them, won't you, Merry?' I did not want her to have them but it would have been churlish to refuse.

'Of course I will. You would not want my personal maid to feel scorn for me when she unpacks my belongings, would you, Elizabeth?'

'No,' I sighed, and went upstairs to fetch my necklace.

★ ★ ★

Merry looked lovely that last morning. She wore turquoise silk with a matching hat perched on top of her curls, white slippers, and kid gloves with pearl buttons at the wrists. She also wore my pearls and promised again to return them the moment Cousin Grace provided her with some jewellery of her own.

Neither Merry nor I had ever travelled by rail, and kind Mr Arthur announced that as it was unseemly for a young lady to travel unescorted by train, he would accompany my sister as he could combine the journey to London with a business engagement, and would see her safely to Cousin Grace's house, which was close to Hyde Park.

I worried about Merry and missed her greatly, for it was the first time we had ever been separated. Would she get on with Cousin Grace? Could she, so immature and scatter-brained, cope with the new pressures which life in the great city would surely thrust upon her?

I was soon to know.

'It is Heaven here, dearest,' she wrote, some three weeks later. 'Cousin Grace is kindness itself and has showered me with clothes and jewels. Money flows like water in this house and 'dearest Cedric' made certain that his wife should want for nothing.

'If you could but see the rooms here, Elizabeth, and all the sumptuous furnishings! Cousin Grace owns two carriages and there are any amount of servants in the house and grooms in the stables. On fine days we take the air in a landau, and Elizabeth, last week I saw the Princess of Wales in the Park and she smiled at me as if I were a friend!'

'Stuff and nonsense,' grunted Father, as I paused for breath, 'the child's head is well and truly turned.'

'And Cousin Grace is out of mourning now,' I read on, 'and beginning to give supper parties so that I can be introduced. She has no important contacts, 'dearest Cedric' was only a tradesman, after all, so I do not know why she looked down upon our mother. But she is a Sponsor of the Arts, dearest, and I have met a fascinating man. His name is Lucas Silver and he is a magician.'

My hands dropped to my lap as I stared at Father. 'A magician!'

'Always was an empty-headed little goose, young Grace,' he muttered, 'just as well she and your mother never met — they would never have got on.'

I was quite certain that my father's cousin was not the right sort of chaperone for my frivolous sister. A magician, indeed! What was the lady thinking of?

That autumn of 'seventy-eight I went to London. After receiving further ecstatic letters from Merry, informing us that she was now helping Mr Silver in his Act, actually *performing* in front of people, I could bear it no longer. Father and I decided that I would have to travel to Hyde Park and see for myself exactly what was going on, and Mrs Stubbs agreed to come and stay with Father for three days.

So I ventured forth in my navy costume, taking a deep red silk for evening which I had inherited from Mother, and had refurbished with an attractive lace collar. Unlike Merry, my clothes did not bother me; I went to observe rather than be observed, and wanted only to be sure that all was well with my sister and that she was in control of her foolish little head.

It did not perturb me that I had to travel alone. Such behaviour might be unseemly, but I was neither a high-born lady, nor a young Miss straight from the schoolroom. It was imperative that I see Merry at once and ascertain what was happening in Cousin Grace's extraordinary household.

2

If I had been clever and experienced, a worldly woman, it might have been easier for me to deal with a man like Lucas Silver. But I was simply a girl from the country, seeing both my dear sister and my foolish cousin ensnared in the man's web. He was evil, I was sure of it, but he behaved impeccably and possessed an aura of mystique which intrigued everyone he met.

I do not think that men liked him, but they respected him and were, perhaps, a little afraid. Even Pitts, the butler, who was trained never to show his feelings, moved with undue haste to serve Lucas Silver; yet there was something in his expression which told me that he did not care for the man.

Mr Silver was living with Cousin Grace as guest of honour, and he occupied a suite of rooms on the third floor where he slept and practised his arts.

At first I did not believe that there was any magic in him, it was surely all tricks and illusions? Yet when his dark eyes stared into mine I felt a shiver go through me, and had the strong conviction that with him anything was possible.

During dinner on that first evening, conversation was held almost in whispers between Merry, Cousin Grace and myself, for Mr Silver remained silent. It seemed that he was not a man of words and if he did not utter it was an affront to him if anyone else broke the silence.

After the meal we three women retired to Cousin Grace's pink and silver sitting-room.

'Mr Silver will be joining us later,' she informed me, 'but first he likes to meditate a while.'

Then I was asked about Father and my journey there, and told about the week-end's events.

'I am having a dinner party tomorrow, Elizabeth, and Mr Silver will entertain us afterwards. You must see him perform whilst you are with us, he is quite brilliant, you know.'

My cousin's big blue eyes shone with admiration and her voice took on a reverent hush when she spoke his name. She was a small, very round lady, and it was obvious that she ate too well and exercised too little. She also had a preference for pastel shades which accentuated her bulk.

Merry looked radiant, as slim as ever and with a glow to her skin which had not been apparent before. The London air must be doing her good, or was it Mr Silver's influence?

'What an unusual looking man,' I remarked, as we sat with our embroidery, waiting for him to join us. 'Do you know anything about his background, Cousin Grace?'

'Most interesting, dear,' she said in a low voice, putting aside her sewing. 'Mr Silver was introduced to me by a friend, who knew a friend of his departed father. Of course, everyone knows that I help people with talent and Mr Silver was in need of a sponsor. Poor as a church-mouse, my dear. His father was a clergyman and his mother a gypsy.' She folded her fat little hands together.

'So romantic, Elizabeth,' went on my sister, breathlessly, 'the gypsy girl was found half-dead on the porch of the rectory, apparently abandoned by her people. Nobody knows more than that for she was a deaf mute and did not utter one word for all the time she lived. But the clergyman wanted to help her, so he married her and they had one son — Lucas Silver.'

'Very romantic,' I said, wondering if the tale were true.

'Your sister does not seem to be impressed by that moving story,' remarked a voice, and we all turned to see Mr Silver standing in the doorway.

Merry and Cousin Grace blushed and jumped to their feet, offering him the most comfortable chair beside the fire, re-arranging themselves so that they had a better view of their master's face. I remained where I was, busily sewing.

His voice irritated me; it was deep and resonant and although he spoke quietly I could imagine it having the power to fill a music hall. It was an actor's voice, carefully trained and cultivated, and his clothing was very odd.

Mr Silver wore a long black robe, like a monk's habit, secured by a leather belt. The collar was round, high to his throat, and round his neck hung a silver chain at the end of which was a heavy medallion, the device of which I could not make out. He was heavily bearded and his black hair was long, touching his shoulders. The skin on his hands and face was very white, and his eyes were black and heavy-lidded. It was his eyes which troubled me more than anything else about his extraordinary appearance.

''Tis a sad story,' I answered, not

raising my head from my work, 'for I take it that both your parents are now dead?'

'Indeed yes, and although I was educated, for my father had taught me well, I had a hard time making my way in the world. Life does not smile on a man who is penniless, Miss Elizabeth. However, since meeting your cousin, Fate has blessed me and my fortunes have changed for the better.'

'You know I will help you in every way I can,' cried Cousin Grace, rising and placing a bottle of brandy and a glass on the table beside him. 'Mr Silver is already captivating London,' she glanced back at me with a coy smile, 'and later I have plans for him to conquer the New World.'

'The New World?' I echoed.

'May I tell her?'

'Of course.'

'Well,' explained my cousin, coming back to sit beside me, 'my dearest Cedric had a brother living in New York, and William has often asked me to visit him and his family. I should never dare to travel so far on my own but with Mr Silver's company I would have a purpose, and it should not be difficult for William to arrange some parties and introduce Lucas Silver to America!'

Later, in our bedroom, I discussed Mr Silver with Merry. Indeed, he was the sole topic of my thoughts, and of every conversation during my stay in London.

'Is he not handsome, Elizabeth?' asked my sister, as she sat on the bed in her frilled nightgown, looking like an excited child.

We were sharing a room which had an enormous four-poster in the centre, large enough to sleep a family. Cousin Grace had suggested that I sleep with Merry in order to see as much of her as possible and, indeed, it was the only time that we managed to have a private conversation.

'I cannot say that I find Mr Silver handsome,' I answered Merry carefully, 'but he is certainly a most striking man. What an odd way to earn a living, though. Does he get paid for these performances?'

'Oh, yes. He lives here quite free of charge, of course, and Cousin Grace pays him every time he entertains her friends. He is also invited to other houses, Elizabeth, and I believe he receives five pounds for each performance. Imagine that!'

I nodded. It did seem an incredible sum but I could not like the man. Better by far to be an honest clergyman existing on half-pence and his parishioners' prayers, than behaving in this weird fashion. I said as much to my sister but she would have none of it.

'Mr Silver pleases people, he entertains and gives much amusement. What clergyman preaching at his flock gives pleasure, or happiness? People come away from the Silver performances smiling and intrigued, you cannot say the same of the prim and pompous church-goers, Elizabeth.'

She had matured, my sister, even in the short time she had been away, and her use of words was amazing. Where had she gained this knowledge? From Lucas Silver who spoke so little? Or from her woman's heart which leapt to defend a lover? I quailed at the thought and slept badly.

Mr Silver neither amused me, nor gave me pleasure, but I was worried by him and also frightened. Merry was too much under his spell, helping him in so many of his tricks that I looked across at Cousin Grace wanting to call out, no, don't let her do it. Not again. But my sister was up there with the man, on my second evening in London, in an alcove backed by red velvet curtains. She had changed into a robe of flimsy white material, looking Grecian in style, which flowed from her narrow shoulders in soft straight folds to her ankles.

The hushed audience sat on every available chair in the long drawing-room, and on the two sofas; whilst more gentlemen crowded in at the back, some on tip-toe, all totally absorbed, whilst I sat tucked away at the side, filled with unease.

Silver stood for a moment facing the room, his head thrown back, then he raised his arms outstretched on either side of his body and his deep voice rang out.

'Ladies and gentlemen, I intend showing you the power of the mind when it is properly trained. Most of us have this power to a greater or lesser extent, but few have learned to discipline it and use its considerable strength. If you could channel this force you would have, as I do, power over pain, power to deal with problems, indeed,' and his teeth gleamed momentarily in the darkness of his beard, 'power over people.'

First he asked the audience if there was anyone present who feared some special thing.

One young girl put up her hand. 'Mice,' she said, and gave a nervous giggle.

'Birds,' announced an elderly lady, shivering.

'Spiders,' said another.

'Are none of the gentlemen here afraid of anything?' asked Mr Silver, his dark eyes searching the room. 'We must have a courageous lot tonight.'

There was a ripple of laughter and a shuffling of feet, but nobody answered him.

'I believe there is one amongst you who has a great dread of reptiles — will she not come forward?' I heard him say.

Nobody moved and I stared down at my shoes which showed beneath the hem of my skirt. My heart was beating furiously as I willed myself to keep calm, to control the tell-tale colour which was flooding my cheeks. How did he know? Merry did not, nor did my father, unless Mother had told him. Once, long ago, we had been walking in the fields, Mother and I, and a thin green grass snake had crossed our path. Although only a child at the time, I can still remember the panic, the overwhelming terror which had rooted me to the spot until the reptile had slithered away out of sight. Mother had taken me up into her arms and comforted me, and I had begged her never to tell anyone of my fear. Even then I had been stubborn and proud of my good sense, and could not bear that anyone should hear of this weakness and perhaps mock me for it.

Since that time, any picture of a snake had made me feel quite ill, but I had fortunately never seen another living one.

How did this man know? I was appalled by his knowledge yet determined not to draw attention to myself, nor to admit that he was right. After a moment's silence he spoke again, and I could relax.

'Very well,' said Lucas Silver, 'perhaps the ladies who feared mice, spiders and birds would come up here and join me?'

I was able to lift my head then and

watch as they moved forward, the younger girls eagerly, the older woman with an apprehensive look on her face.

'Now, madam,' he turned to the elderly lady, 'may I ask you to trust me completely?' She nodded. 'Then give me your hands and look into my eyes.' Silver bent slightly forward and gazed into his companion's face. Then, very slowly, he said, 'You like birds; you like the flutter of their wings, and their curved claws; you will never be frightened of a bird again. Say that after me.'

Softly, hesitantly, she repeated what the man had said, her eyes all the while fixed on his, their hands interlocked.

'Now,' Silver straightened, letting go of her hands. 'I am going to prove to you and all these people that what I say is true. You have lost your fear of birds. Meredith,' his voice became louder and he glanced across at my sister who stood, still as a statue, at one side of the alcove. 'Meredith, bring me the doves.'

I saw my sister slip out through the

side door and appear a minute later holding a cage with two white birds in it. She moved across to join the magician, who opened the door of the cage and brought out first one dove and then the other. They fluttered, balancing themselves on his sleeve, then he turned to the woman and held out the birds to her.

'Take them,' he commanded, and she smiled and held out her hands and the birds danced along her fingers, white necks twisting, red eyes gleaming.

'Goodness gracious!' said a startled voice beside me, 'Dorothy cannot abide the creatures. She will not even walk in the park for fear of the sparrows.'

A murmur of astonishment arose from the assembled throng, followed by a burst of applause which sent the birds soaring into the air, circling and flapping in confusion.

'Snow! Princess! Come here.' Silver's voice rang out, and he took the cage and held it high above his head. 'Come, my beauties.'

The frightened creatures swooped, one to the cage, the other to his shoulder, then he returned them gently to their home amidst more feverish clapping.

After handing the cage back to Merry, who withdrew with it, he turned to one of the younger girls.

'As for you, my little one, you will never be afraid of mice again.'

The magician placed his hand lightly on her head, as if in benediction, and she, gazing up into his face, repeated similar words to the ones we had heard before. Both she and her companion were shown mice and spiders, carried into the room in small boxes by Merry, and it did indeed appear as if Mr Silver had helped them to banish fear.

'I will now show you another example, ladies and gentlemen,' announced Silver, once the three ladies had returned to their seats, 'of power over people. Would some of you be good enough to write a name or a date on a piece of paper and hand it to my assistant? She will then stand at the far end of the room and read what you have written, keeping that knowledge to herself. But whilst she thinks of the word or set of figures, I shall endeavour to read her mind and announce to you all what is written on the paper she holds.'

There was sudden movement and chatter amongst the guests, as Cousin Grace fussed about in her blue and white flounces, offering pencils and strips of note-paper, and Merry moved amongst us, smiling and collecting up the white strips.

'Write something, Elizabeth, he is so good at this it will astound you,' she said, moving to my side.

'No.' I shook my head, determined not to be included in any part of the man's trickery. 'I am here to observe, not participate.'

She shrugged, then returned to the alcove, placing the papers on a small table beside her. Silver stood right away from her by the opposite wall, and it was clearly impossible for him to see what Merry held in her hands.

Astounding it certainly was. Merry would pick up one sheet after another and study it before closing her eyes, and Lucas Silver would instantly speak a name or a number; to prove that it was entirely genuine, he then asked the audience,

'Who wrote that?'

And both gentlemen and ladies, with astonishment plain on their faces, answered, 'I did.'

I could not see how such thought-reading could be faked, and a cold tide of panic rose in my stomach as I realised the true power of the man, and the appalling dominance he could have over people's lives.

Merry must get away from him, she must leave London before it was too late. But how could I pit my wits against such a being? What control could I have over Merry now that she was within the awesome clutches of Mr Lucas Silver?

The final act only increased my trepidation. I saw Silver draw forward three upright chairs and place them in a row; saw him speaking to my sister, so quietly that it was impossible to hear what he was saying but it was obvious that he was sending her into a trance.

Stiltedly, like a wooden doll, she seated herself sideways upon the centre chair, then the magician lifted her feet and placed them on the side chair and she lay back with her head and neck supported by the other. He bent over her then, the silver medallion swinging from his chest, catching the light, as he talked softly.

The big drawing-room was hushed, the thirty or forty guests unmoving, scarcely breathing, for this was Silver's grand finale, the moment they had all been anticipating.

My hands were clenched tightly into the folds of my gown, and I could feel my nails cutting into my palms as I sat rigid, watching the black figure bowed over my sister's inert form.

The man straightened and remained absolutely still for a moment, staring down at his victim, then he moved round to the back of her and removed first the centre chair, then the one beneath her feet, finally the one supporting her head.

A great sigh went up from the audience as we perceived Merry's body lying on air.

With a swift movement Silver replaced the chairs, two at once beneath her body, the last for her head, and as the crowd burst into cheering and clapping, he rubbed Merry's hands, talking to her until she opened her eyes.

Helping her to her feet he stood beside her, bowing and smiling, but my sister looked pale and tired, and I saw a sheen of perspiration on Silver's forehead. The concentration for such an effort must have been immense, and the couple slipped quickly away through the side door as Cousin Grace brought the evening to a close with a few trite remarks.

I felt exhausted myself, and went hastily up to our room hoping that Merry would be safely there. She was, hurriedly disrobing, her hands shaking as she flung the white dress from her. But she would not discuss the performance.

'Leave me in peace, Elizabeth, I must sleep. Mr Silver and I are always greatly fatigued by the end of our act. Join me, if you are also weary, but do not talk, I beg.'

The following morning I awoke early; in fact my three nights in London were marred by dreams and constant awakenings, although Merry was not disturbed and slept peacefully beside me.

I went for a walk that Sunday, letting myself out of the house to the consternation of a little maid who was unused to seeing anyone downstairs at that hour of the morning.

There was a small square nearby with

a church neatly placed within it, and I felt in need of repose and a sense of security. We were not church-going people, but I stepped into the building hoping that the sound of prayers would comfort me.

But as I watched the clergyman up at the altar he reminded me of Lucas Silver, and the voice which rang out was the voice of the magician. I stared in dismay at the black-robed man, and although his hair was white and his face benevolent, my fears remained. The service did not help me and I hurried out, once it was over, to breathe deeply of the fresh cold air.

Just before reaching Cousin Grace's house, I felt a touch on my arm and turning, saw a thin, poorly garbed woman at my side. Her skin had a greyish tinge to it, and although her hair was covered with a ragged shawl, I could tell that she was old, old and sick.

'Please, ma'am.' She plucked at my sleeve, clutching a bundle to her chest with the other.

'What is it?' I stared down at her, wanting to shake myself free from such wretchedness, yet feeling a pity which I could not hide. 'What do you want from me? I have no money.'

She shook her head quickly. 'I do not beg money from you, but you have a kind face, ma'am, and I am in desperate need of help. Not from you,' she added hastily, 'but from Mr Silver, ma'am. Please give him a message from me.'

She was not badly spoken and must have seen better days, but now her feet were bare, stained with mud and filth, as was the hem of her shabby gown. As we spoke, the mite in her arms let out a sickly wail and my companion rocked it closer to her breast, all the while staring at me with her great sunken eyes.

'I do not ask for myself, ma'am, but for Lucy, here. She is right poorly and I need money for her and little Susie back home. I've tried asking at the door, but that butler won't let me in, and I know my messages aren't getting

41

through to Mr Silver, for I've been calling and waiting here every day for a week, and he has not come out to see me. Tell him it's urgent, ma'am. Lucy must have proper medicine or she'll die.'

A slow tear rolled down the woman's cheek and I realised with a shock that she was probably not much older than I was.

'I have no money or I'd gladly give you some.' I had only enough for my fare home, but possibly Cousin Grace would help this poor creature. 'I do not know if Mr Silver will listen to me, he is a strange man. Why do you want to speak to him?'

Had she heard of his powers and imagined in her ignorance that he was a new Messiah, able to help the poor and needy?

'I shall ask my cousin to assist you.' I turned, about to return to the house.

'No, no, I do not want charity!' The woman's face flushed and her lips tightened. 'I ask only what is my right, and the father of my children should

make it his duty to provide for them
— especially now that he is doing so
well for himself.' She lifted her chin. 'I
do not ask for myself, ma'am, on my
own I could cope well enough. But 'tis
for the little ones. Tell him that, ma'am.
We live at the same address and he has
only to send there. Tell him a few
shillings will do then I'll not be
bothering him again.'

My mouth had fallen open in
astonishment as she spoke, and I could
feel my heart beginning to hammer
within my chest.

'Do you mean that Mr Silver is the
father of this child?' I asked hoarsely.

She nodded. 'And of Susie back
home. We was married nigh on five
years ago, ma'am, but now he's risen
above us and I'm right glad for him,
he's ever so clever and I won't stand in
his way. I'll leave him alone in future,
tell him that, but I must have help now
for the little ones.'

I nodded fiercely, my hands clench-
ing, as I realised how Merry and

Cousin Grace had been duped. Rage burned in my bosom as I turned quickly, beginning to move back along the pavement.

'I shall make it my business to see that Mr Silver hears from my own lips about you, and you will get your money, I vouch for that.'

'Bless you, ma'am.' Her voice reached me faintly as I strode back to Cousin Grace's house and hurried up the front steps.

The same little maid let me in and whispered that a fire had been lit in the front drawing-room, and she would bring me breakfast there.

'I desire nothing,' I said through my teeth, wanting only to face Mr Silver with my newly acquired information and denounce him in front of my family. 'Are the others still a-bed? What time do they rise on a Sunday?'

'Not until noon, ma'am.' The little maid bobbed. 'But Mr Silver is usually down early and takes his breakfast in the front room.'

'Very well. I shall wait for him there.'

I swept up the stairs to the room on the first floor, anxious to confront the man as soon as possible.

He joined me soon afterwards, pausing for a moment with his back to the door, his eyes surveying me coolly as I paced the carpet.

'I have just returned from a meeting with your wife, Mr Silver,' I said loudly, clasping my hands before me and standing to return his gaze. 'The baby is ill and she needs money for both your children.'

He raised his eyebrows, a half-smile curving his lips beneath his beard. 'I am afraid I do not know what you are talking about, Miss Elizabeth,' he said in his deep voice, moving across the room towards me. 'Come, let us sit down and partake of some refreshment. I do not believe you slept well, and doubtless some dream still lingers in your tired mind.'

'I did not dream this meeting, Mr Silver, and am not as innocent and trusting as my sister. I saw your wife and youngest child but a few minutes ago, and Mrs Silver asked me to speak to you on her behalf.'

'Miss Elizabeth — I have no wife.' He seated himself upon the velvet sofa, his eyes remaining steady on my face, but I turned my back and walked over to the window.

'You cannot disconcert me, sir, and I am afraid neither Cousin Grace nor Merry will be pleased by what I have to tell them.' My hand went up to move the lace curtains to one side. 'She is waiting in the street for you to go down and see her, I promised that I would pass on her message — you cannot refuse to — '

Momentarily I paused, catching my breath, for the pavement beneath was deserted and there was no one in sight.

'Is she there — this wife of mine?' The amusement in his voice riled me, and I turned sharply, allowing the curtain to fall back into place. 'No doubt she has returned home. But I promised to aid her, Mr Silver, and I always keep my word.'

'Then that was a foolish thing to do,' he said softly, 'for I assure you that I have no wife. You must have met with a beggar woman who made up this story in order to stir your tender heart. Have a care, Miss Elizabeth, I can see much trouble ahead for you if you do not learn to curb your emotions.'

'I promised!' The woman's pleading eyes remained vivid in my mind, and her poor lined face, and naked feet. 'And I believed her. Tell me her address, sir, if you will not aid her, and I shall beg help from Cousin Grace and go to her myself.'

'I do not know the woman and have no idea where she might live.' He rang the bell beside him and then sat back. 'Let us forget this unfortunate episode and break bread together in peace. You and I have much in common, Miss Elizabeth, and I want to know you better. I have the feeling that our lives are to be linked in future, and it would be better for us both if we can learn to like and understand each other.'

I faced him stormily. 'That is out of the question. You are a cruel, heartless man, Mr Silver, and I shall not rest until Merry is free from your clutches and safely home with Father and me.'

He laughed then, his teeth showing white through his beard. 'What formidable opponents — a sick man and a young emotional girl! Go, Miss Elizabeth, by all means, tell your tale to sister Meredith, but I can assure you that neither she nor your cousin will believe your word against mine.'

Of course they did not, and the following morning, sickened by their devotion to such a man, I left London and returned home. There was nothing I could do for Merry, no way in which I could persuade her to accompany me; she was hopelessly under Lucas Silver's spell. But I hoped that I would be able to get Father to summon her home, and that she would leave Cousin Grace's establishment forever.

3

I returned home after that disturbing week-end in London determined to explain to Father about Merry's unsuitable alliance with Lucas Silver, and beg him to order her home at once. But on my return I discovered that Father had suffered a relapse and I was greeted by a scared Mrs Stubbs and the constant visits of Dr Poole. He told me that there was little hope for my father, but with complete rest and careful nursing he might last a few more months. All thoughts of Merry left me, and I shared day and night watches with Mrs Stubbs as we fought to prolong Father's life. I was always thankful not to have mentioned Merry's association with Mr Silver, for Father died in that June of 'seventy-nine, but he died with his mind at rest.

There were only a few people at the

funeral, but some beautiful flowers were donated which helped to relieve the dreariness of the plain wood coffin and the black-garbed mourners. Cousin Grace came, and Merry, of course, and also Lucas Silver.

What right had he to intrude upon our private grief, adding to my distress with his sinister presence? Had Merry begged him to come? Or was Cousin Grace incapable of moving without her long-gowned shadow?

Mr Silver held my hands for a moment, murmuring condolence which I did not wish to hear from his lips, and, avoiding his eyes, I gazed down at the silver medallion on his chest. But immediately I turned my head away and snatched my hands from his grasp, for the design was of a coiled serpent, with its head arising from the body mass and its evil forked tongue protruding from its flat head.

'I should have worn it face down, forgive me for upsetting you.'

There was amusement in his voice

and I turned away in panic, seeking Miss Bloster, or Mr Drew, anyone who was normal and with whom I could feel at ease.

They all came back to the house for refreshments afterwards, and then it was that I looked at Merry for the first time that day and was shocked by her appearance. We had both worn veils at the church, but once home both these and our hats were set aside and I thought how very pale Merry had become, and thinner than ever. Although we had both wept tears enough her pallor was alarming, and I could not believe that it was caused solely by her distress over Father.

'What ails you, Merry?' I asked out in the kitchen, as we cleared away the dishes before our guests made ready to depart. 'Are you not well? It is so long since I last saw you and can see a dreadful change. What is wrong?'

Her eyes brimmed with tears again. 'So much has happened, Elizabeth, I cannot tell you now but I shall write.'

She glanced hastily at the door and was ill-at-ease. 'I may be coming home soon, you would not mind that?'

'Of course not, this is your home just as much as it is mine. Are you sick, Merry? Is it that devil Lucas Silver? Is he upsetting you?'

'No, no.' She smiled through her tears and fumbled for her handkerchief. 'I shall write, Elizabeth, say no more for now. But I shall be coming and we'll have a happy time together, just for a while, dearest.'

She kissed me briefly then went back to join the company gathered in the hallway.

After waving away the carriage belonging to Cousin Grace, I returned to the house, to find Miss Bloster waiting for me.

'I shall not keep you long, Elizabeth, as I know you must be weary, but there is something I wish to say. Money matters will doubtless begin to worry you once you have overcome your distress, and your father's pension will now cease. All I want to say is that I am in need of assistance at the school and would gladly have you in my employ, if the idea appeals to you.'

I thanked her as best I could, and was overwhelmed when she bent and placed her wrinkled cheek against mine.

'You are a good girl, Elizabeth, and your mother would have been proud of you.'

I began teaching the little ones at Miss Bloster's establishment the following week; money was indeed short and besides that, I was lonely in the house and had not nearly enough to do to fill my days. I quickly grew to love the gaunt, sarcastic woman, whose life was her school, and whose one aim was to send her girls out into the world wiser, and more competent, human beings.

Miss Bloster worshipped knowledge and believed that every female should be able to hold a decent conversation with a man, and that good deportment, music and painting were not adequate accomplishments.

'Of course that is all the parents desire and I must comply with their wishes,' she told me, 'but my girls know more than that, Elizabeth, when they leave me. I have had Madame Lavelle lecture them on the Franco-Prussian war. She is a refugee, poor dear, and I do not suppose she enjoyed remembering. But her personal experiences brought home to my pupils all the horror and mess of war far more than any history book would have done. We have also been thoroughly into the Crimean War, and as several of the girls' fathers were involved, doubtless more questions were asked at home once the children's interest was fired.'

'I remember studying Lord Tennyson's excellent poem 'The Charge of the Light Brigade' with you,' I acknowledged, 'and can still repeat it, line for line.'

'Your memory was always good.' She nodded. 'These things *are* history, child, and mean more to my girls than silly tales of Alfred burning the cakes, or Canute ordering the waves to stand still.'

Miss Bloster had great faith in the future of women.

'One day, Elizabeth, women will be able to hold equal positions with men in Government, in the law courts, and in medicine. Men have had their own way for too long and I am beginning to see a glimmer of hope for our future. We now have women undergraduates at Cambridge, and the London School of Medicine for Women. Our Queen is a fine example of our sex, but then Britain has always been fair about Royalty. Now this equality must be carried through to the ordinary people.'

There were more pupils now than when Merry and I attended, thirty girls in all, and Miss Bloster was enthusiastic, inspired by the parents who were willing to have their daughters educated as well as their sons, and who wished their girls to mingle with others instead of living the restricted life of private lessons and governesses.

I became imbued with Miss Bloster's fervour, deciding that here was the sort of work which I could put my heart into, knowing, too, that it would help me more quickly to get over Father's death and the worry of my sister's strange life.

Thoughts of Merry and Lucas Silver troubled me often but there was nothing I could do until Merry chose to write. If she did decide to return home, I did not believe that my work would disrupt her visit. My hours were from nine-thirty until noon, and then from two-thirty until three-thirty. As I lived but a ten minute walk from Miss Bloster's establishment, I always returned for my mid-day meal, and this meant that Merry and I could lunch together, and then she could doubtless fill up her mornings with a little housework and shopping.

Mr Arthur Drew still called by some evenings, and as we both enjoyed reading the same kind of books, I looked forward to his visits. It did not occur to me that he would have any other reason for calling, but some weeks after Father's death he proposed to me.

'It is not right that you should be living here all alone, nor working so hard at that school,' he said. 'If you would honour me with your hand in marriage, Miss Elizabeth, I should be a happy man.'

This was said with such sombre countenance that I almost smiled. Dearly as I should have liked to marry and have children, I could not see myself living with Mr Arthur for the rest of my life. I felt nothing save mild affection for him, and suspected that his mournful appearance would soon irritate me.

'I am deeply honoured, Mr Drew,' I began carefully, 'and had no idea that you cared for me, having always imagined that your affections were for my sister.'

'I was, and am, very fond of Meredith, Miss Elizabeth,' he said earnestly, 'but since she went to London she has only had eyes for Mr Silver. A strange man, I fear, and not one with whom a young lady should be associating.' His look became severe. 'But doubtless your cousin is caring for Meredith and seeing that she comes to no harm.'

'I think Cousin Grace is equally infatuated with the man, Mr Drew, but Merry tells me that she will be coming home soon and I shall be thankful to have her safely with me again.'

His face brightened. 'That is good news. But you have not answered my question, Miss Elizabeth, and I should like a reply for Mother is anxious to see me wed.'

He preferred Merry, but as she was no longer available he would take me in order to please his mother.

'May I ask for some time in which to think the matter over, Mr Drew? Marriage is not something which can be taken lightly and I should like time in which to consider.'

I knew in my heart that this was not the right man for me; I longed for a love-match, the kind of partnership which my parents had shared. But if Mr Drew's offer was refused, what other chance would I ever have?

'Certainly, Miss Elizabeth.' He rose to his feet and bowed over my hand. 'I shall call again in a week, or so, for your answer.'

Late one afternoon in August Merry returned.

She travelled down alone in Cousin Grace's carriage which appeared to overflow with her numerous boxes and baskets and trunks. After John, the coachman, had carried her pieces upstairs and been rewarded with a hot meat pie and a cup of tea, he departed on his return journey leaving my sister and me companionably on our own for the first time in months.

'This is grand,' I announced, as we partook of the pies which I had baked that morning, it being a Saturday and thus a free day for me. 'You are looking so much better, Merry, I do believe you have put on weight at last. How long can you stay? I do hope it will not be for a mere couple of weeks.'

Secretly I was hoping that her stay would become permanent, but I dared not voice my opinions too soon.

'Indeed no.' She smiled in a curious fashion and nibbled elegantly at her pie-crust. 'Your pastry is as good as ever, Elizabeth, you inherited that gift from Mother whilst I can scarcely cook an egg without ruining it.'

'Only for want of practise. Perhaps you would like to try your hand at preparing some meals? It would help me as I am away from the house for most of the day.'

'You go out to work?' She glanced at me sharply. 'I did not know that. What do you do, Elizabeth? Is it necessary?'

'I help Miss Bloster at the school, and I'm afraid it is. Father left me the house and his small savings, but they are not enough to keep me.'

Merry tapped her fingers against the

table and I thought how lovely she looked, with colour in her face once more, and her cheeks rounded out and her eyes seeming a deeper blue than before.

'I hope this will not inconvenience you, Elizabeth, but I shall be staying half a year with you, at least until February.'

'That is splendid,' I said warmly. After six months she would have forgotten all about Mr Silver and perhaps Mr Drew could be persuaded to turn his affections from me to my sister.

'You see,' Merry went on, 'Cousin Grace and Lucas are off to America at the end of the month and will not return until the spring.'

'Why do you not go with them? Have you quarrelled with Mr Silver?' I asked hopefully.

'No, no, nothing like that. I love Lucas and he loves me, as you have probably guessed. But I cannot travel with them because I am with child.'

At this announcement the blood drained from my face and I felt quite faint. 'Merry!'

'You will get used to the idea eventually,' stated my sister, licking her fingers. 'We will marry, of course, but there is much against us at present.'

'How could you behave in such a shameful manner! And what would Mother have said?' I was appalled by the news and the calm way in which Merry helped herself to another pie. 'You ought to be whipped for such behaviour, and Mr Silver — Mr Silver must — '

'Elizabeth, calm yourself and listen to me. We cannot marry yet because Cousin Grace is a jealous old cat and could not bear to know that Lucas loves me. She is sure to leave him all her money when she dies, but if we act hastily she will quite likely cut him out of her will all together. We must be very careful, Elizabeth, and do nothing to arouse her suspicions. So that is why I am here and the reason Lucas cleverly arranged the American trip at this time. On their return to London I shall go back and continue assisting him, as slim and unburdened as I was before.'

'Merry, this is too much!' I scraped back my chair and began to pace the kitchen. 'What of your baby, what do you intend doing with it? And what about the wife and family that devil already possesses?'

My sister stared at me coldly. 'Lucas has no wife. I wish you would not bring up that subject. And you are to keep this child, Elizabeth, until such a time as we can claim it as our own.'

I placed my hands on my hips and stared grimly back. 'Tomorrow I intend going up to London and putting the whole case before Cousin Grace. She is responsible for you, seeing that you were in her care when this dreadful thing happened, and it is about time she realised what a blackguard her precious Lucas Silver is!'

'I would not do that if I were you,' answered my sister. 'Lucas has planned most carefully and I should not like to see his wrath provoked. He is a very powerful man, Elizabeth, you have seen that for yourself, and I do not want to see you hurt.'

There was a stillness about her, a deadly seriousness, which perturbed me and, remembering the black-gowned man who was her lover, and the father of her unborn child, I shivered.

'It will not be for long,' Merry said more gently, 'and then I shall go away and leave you in peace. And you love babies, Elizabeth, it will surely not be too much to ask? Do not despair, Cousin Grace's health is not very good and I doubt that she will live longer than a year, or so. Then we will be free to wed and will take our child and not worry you any more.' She yawned, stretching her arms above her head. 'That journey tired me more than I knew, I must go and sleep. Am I to have my old room? How strange it will be — back in the nest once more. Is the bed made up and ready for me?'

'I prepared everything when I got your letter. Go to bed now and allow me time to think, your arrival here is not the happy event which I was anticipating.'

We had quarrelled as children, Merry and I, but since Mother's death I had accepted the responsibility of my family and had enjoyed mothering my small sister. It was difficult to believe that this foolish, uncaring creature was the girl whom I had cherished but a few months back. No doubt Silver's influence was responsible for more than the one change in her, but I wondered dismally how we would get on together during the next six months, and how I could ever break his hold over her now that she was bearing his child.

The next morning Merry and I made our plans. At least I planned, and my sister listened to my suggestions; she did not appear interested in what I had to say but I persevered, determined to hold my temper in check. If we were to live under the same roof arguments and an unpleasant atmosphere would not help at all.

For the time being I had decided to do as she asked — give her a home and eventually take care of her baby. For the moment that was all that I could promise, I would worry about the future at a later date. Somehow a way would have to be found to keep both Merry and the child away from Lucas Silver.

'First of all you must wear a wedding ring,' I announced. 'Mother's is still upstairs in my box and you can wear that whilst you are here.'

'Why?' asked Merry, hands idle in her lap as she lolled in the old rocking chair.

'Because people will talk if you do not.'

'That worries me not at all,' said Merry. 'I shall be here but for a short time, who cares if the old bodies wag their tongues? It will liven their dreary lives a bit.'

'I care! It is all very well for you to

leave in the spring and go back to your life of wealth and comforts, but I shall remain here, and so will your child. Have a thought for someone other than yourself for a change.'

'Poor Elizabeth, do not bite my head off, dearest. You sound as embittered as Miss Bloster. What a pity you have not found yourself a husband. I dread to think what you will be like after a few more years of spinsterhood, living in this Godforsaken corner of the world. Still,' she shrugged, 'as you will, Elizabeth, you are mistress here and if it will ease your conscience I shall sport Mother's ring for all to see.'

'Thank you.' I spoke quietly, gripping the table to steady my hands. 'You will have to say that you and Mr Silver were wed in London last April, and that you did not inform me because I do not like the man. That at least is the truth. Now your husband has gone to America to further his career, whilst you await the birth of your child.' I put my hand to my head which was beginning to throb.

'Do you ever see Mr Arthur these days?' Merry changed the subject. 'I remember seeing him at Father's funeral and he was kind about calling and visiting him when he was sick.'

'Yes,' I said. 'In fact he has asked me to marry him.' Her taunts about my single state had hurt.

'Mr Arthur wants to marry you?' She let out a small burst of laughter.

'What is so comical about that? He is a considerate and well-mannered gentleman, and Father always said that I would make a good wife.'

'Yes, but not to one so thin, so meek and fastidious as he.' She leaned forward with her elbows on the table. 'You must have a big, burly farmer, Elizabeth, someone who will not stand for your bossy ways. There! I did not mean to hurt you, dearest, but Mr Arthur Drew is not the man for you.'

I had known this for some time but disliked the mockery in my sister's voice and wondered why we should not find happiness together. Our union would be no more peculiar than Merry's with Mr Lucas Silver.

'I have not given him an answer yet,' I replied stiffly, 'but 'tis highly likely that I shall accept his offer.'

I need not have pondered about my future, however, for Merry took control of the situation. When Mr Arthur called the following Wednesday, Merry flirted quite outrageously with him and I saw in his spaniel's eyes all the love and dumb devotion which he would never feel for me. It was not kind of her to behave thus but it proved to me how impossible marriage with such a man would be; anyone who could not see the calculation beneath her fluttering eye-lashes, nor hear the falsity of her tinkling laughter, was a fool. And I did not suffer fools gladly.

Once Merry's condition became apparent, and we informed Mr Arthur that I should be looking after the babe until Merry and Mr Silver were more settled in life, a strained expression appeared on Arthur Drew's face. I allowed him to suffer for a while, then told him gently but firmly that I had considered his proposal most carefully and must regretfully refuse. His relief was so comic that I could not feel insulted, and he soon stopped calling which pleased me but not my sister.

Occasionally letters arrived from America and Merry informed me that Mr Silver's tour was a wild success, and that he and Arabella and Cousin Grace were being entertained lavishly by their cordial American hosts.

'Arabella?' I queried. 'Who is she?'

'His new assistant, and not nearly as good as me, but Lucas had to engage *somebody* for these six months.'

'How did you explain to Cousin Grace that you would not be travelling with them? Was she not suspicious?'

'Lucas said that you were lonely without Father and needed my company for a while. Oh, drat the baby!' she snapped, rustling the pages of her letter. 'I should have been there with them, enjoying all the praise and fun.

There's a message for you, Elizabeth. Lucas tells me to remain with you once our son is born and then he will come down and fetch me as soon as he returns to England. He says that he admires your spirit, and can think of no one better to whom he would entrust his son's care and early upbringing. There — you cannot dislike him so much after that.'

I could and did, and found myself frequently thinking of his other family, and the little girls whom he had refused to acknowledge.

* * *

Merry became more and more bored as the year dragged on. Once Mr Arthur stopped calling she was left to her own devices and she was woefully lacking in resources. Kind Mrs Stubbs called round once a week for a chat, but her life revolved around the town and local gossip was no longer of interest to Merry. She sewed a great deal and wrote numerous letters to Mr Silver, but as she grew larger she also grew lazier, and I would often return home to find her in the rocking-chair, asleep.

Merry used any excuse not to bestir herself, yet expected meals to be ready on time and all her washing and ironing to be done for her. Her own room she kept cleaned and dusted, on my insistence, but otherwise she did little all day save complain that she was bored.

'I do miss London so,' she exclaimed one day, 'you are buried alive down here and I do not know how I stood it before.'

'You were innocent and unspoilt but a few months back,' I told her, 'and would have remained so had it not been for Cousin Grace and her letter of invitation.'

'But then I should not have met Lucas, dearest. Did I tell you that he intends touring the continent on his return?' she went on more brightly. 'And this time I shall travel with him whether Cousin Grace likes it, or not.'

'More travelling? What a restless man he is.'

'Not restless — ambitious. He has a great desire to visit Germany. Lucas admires the Prussians enormously, they are a powerful race, he says, and we should learn more from them.'

'Power, that seems to be his God!' I snapped. 'Does he not care for anything else?'

'Praise and adulation and success — but these will all come to him because of his powers. And he deserves success, Elizabeth. He has had to fight all his life for what he wants and he'll get there in the end, you wait and see.'

'Get where?'

'To the Court, to be adviser to the King.'

'What on earth do you mean? Queen Victoria is on the throne.'

'But the Prince of Wales will one day be King of Britain, dearest, and Lucas says the old Queen should abdicate now but she is so stubborn that she will not.'

'That's treason!'

Merry laughed. 'Oh, Elizabeth, we do not live in the Middle Ages, that word has no meaning now. Lucas believes in being honest and he says that Edward would make a splendid king. He is broadminded and has a sense of humour, and possesses the common touch; all of which qualities his mother lacks.'

'How can Mr Silver contemplate knowing him, let alone advising him? He is a mere nobody, and lowly bred, at that.'

'Lucas has already met the Prince and they got on capitally together. The Prince is fascinated by Lucas and his powers and wants to know more. But Lucas says it is best to remain cool and keep his distance at present. He is playing his cards carefully, Elizabeth, for there are too many people being friendly and begging favours, and that wife of his is a strait-laced creature, not unlike her mother-in-law.'

'Merry! I did not know that you were so well informed. Why did you not tell me? Have you also met the Prince? And why do you not care for Princess Alexandra? She is very beautiful from her photographs.'

'I was introduced to him once when Lucas and I were invited to Marlborough House and performed before the Prince. But I have not met his wife. She does not approve of her husband's friends and I know that she does not like him associating with Lucas. But the Prince is fond of him and we hope for another invitation when Lucas returns.

'You see why I am so bored here, Elizabeth? Lucas has opened up a world that I never knew existed before and he is going to achieve so much, you will be proud of him.'

Proud of him, indeed! I still hated and feared Lucas Silver — God forbid that he should have power near the throne. But the future of Britain and her eventual government was nothing to do with me, whereas Merry's welfare was important and still partly my responsibility. If Mr Silver were to fly so high what need would he have for my flighty little sister? Money, yes. Cousin Grace and her wealth would be essential mixing in such society, but Merry's companionship? He would have no need of that, and my heart turned over as I remembered the poor woman who had pleaded with me outside Cousin Grace's house. If Merry were not very careful she would find herself similarly abandoned.

Strangely, my sister appeared to have no interest in her coming child and would not even discuss names.

'You decide,' she said. 'Unless Lucas writes and tells me that he desires a certain name I really do not care at all. I did not want this baby, Elizabeth, and have no love for children, but Lucas wants it.' She shrugged.

'Then you make a fine pair,' I said, over my sewing, 'for Mr Silver was scarcely a good father to his daughters.'

'Elizabeth — do not go on so about all that rubbish! Lucas told me quite definitely that he had never married. Besides, that woman came from the Work House and was mad.'

I lifted my head. 'What woman?'

'That one who claimed to be his wife,' Merry answered sulkily.

'What do you know about her? What has happened? Tell me at once.' I bent forward gripping her wrist, and she winced and pulled away from me.

'It was nothing, really, just an upsetting incident and Lucas did not want me to tell you. He says you are far too emotional about such matters.'

'You will tell me everything,' I said in a tight voice, 'or I'll not cook you another meal so long as you stay in my house.'

'All right, all right, stop shouting!' Merry pouted, rubbing at her wrist. 'We were going out for a drive, oh, months ago, soon after your visit. And Lucas was driving because he enjoys handling the horses. And Cousin Grace and I were sitting chatting, not paying much attention, and suddenly this — this female flung herself at the carriage and the horses were frightened and they reared up and we were ever so shaken — ' she stopped, her face going white at the memory.

'Go on,' I whispered.

'There was an awful jolt and a bump and somebody screamed, and after Lucas managed to control the horses I looked back and — ' she swallowed, 'and I saw her lying in the road.'

'Dead?' I could hardly make my throat work. 'She was dead?'

Merry nodded. 'And the baby in her arms, also. But the policeman said she was not right in the head, Elizabeth,' she went on quickly, 'and she'd been causing trouble before, and Lucas paid for her funeral so she didn't go to a pauper's grave. But it was not his *fault*, I tell you, she *leapt* out at him and there was no way he could have stopped in time.'

Merry looked at me pleadingly as I

stared back, unable to speak. He had won. Lucas Silver — no, Lucifer! He had rid himself of a tiresome burden and was now free to marry my sister when it pleased him to do so. And free to accept his child, when it suited his plans.

I rose slowly and went to put the kettle on the hob.

'No doubt Mr Silver desires a son?' I said, when I could speak.

'Yes,' said Merry, 'and he says it will be a boy whom he can train to follow him in the act. Lucas has so much knowledge, it must be passed on to the next generation.'

'Then I hope for your sake that the child is a boy, otherwise you may find yourself put aside in the future. Your handsome lover does not appear to care for the females of his family.'

There was one more, somewhere, existing in the slums of London. Susie, that was what the poor woman had called her. A three, or four-year old girl who was now motherless. Or had she also perished?

'I shall take your child, Merry,' I said quietly, 'and care for it, and love it, if I can. And I cannot stop loving you no matter how foolishly you behave. But from now on you will not mention that man's name to me, and he will never be made welcome in this house. Is that understood?'

She nodded, biting her lip, and we did not speak again all evening.

4

Barnaby James Allwood was born on the twenty-sixth of February, 1880, in our back bedroom. Dr Poole attended at his birth, assisted by Mrs Stubbs and me, and although Merry made a terrible fuss and declared that she was going to die, she survived and gave birth to a beautiful baby boy.

He was such a good baby, looking so like Merry with his golden hair and big blue eyes that it was hard to believe that Lucas Silver had sired him. My sister took little notice of him, so he was mine from the moment he was born. She was interested only in getting her figure back to its former slenderness, waiting impatiently for news of Mr Silver and his return to England.

Miss Bloster had been kind and allowed me a month off from work after Barnaby's birth, but after that I took him to school with me, where he slept in an upstairs room and disturbed nobody.

The first sign of impending danger came several weeks after Barnaby was born, as my sister was sorting through her clothes throwing out piles of lovely dresses which were either too old or too small. Merry was fighting hard to recover the eighteen-inch waist which she had once possessed, but it was a weary battle and she was irritable and difficult to live with.

'You will have new clothes once you get back to town,' I said. 'Cousin Grace will set you up once more so do not fret.'

'But I have nothing to travel in,' she wailed, heaving a mass of silks and taffetas onto the floor and kicking the heap with an angry gesture. 'I must look my best for Lucas or he will think I have turned into a country bumpkin.'

'Sit down,' I said soothingly, 'and let me do your hair. It is in a mess but that at least can be quickly remedied.'

'I don't want you touching my hair! You pull it so. And where is my jewel case? Have you taken it?'

'I have not. If you kept everything in better order you would not always be mislaying the objects you require.' As I said this I remembered my pearls. 'You never returned my necklace, Merry, and I should like it when you find your jewel case. Those pearls are the only jewellery I possess apart from my garnet brooch.'

'I haven't got your pearls,' she answered sulkily, flinging herself into the rocking-chair.

'What do you mean? What have you done with them?'

'Lucas took them. He said they needed re-threading and it was to be a surprise for you. I forgot to ask him again, but they will be safe with him, Elizabeth.'

Angrily I hit the table with the flat of my hand. 'They did not need re-threading — they were in perfect

condition. Oh, Merry, how irrespon-
sible of you! You are to inform Mr
Silver the moment he comes back that I
want my pearls immediately. Do you
hear me?'

'There is no need to shout. And why
you make such a fuss about those old
beads I don't know.'

'They were Mother's and very
precious to me. Merry, I could shake
you! Mr Silver has been out of the
country for months and who knows
where they are now?'

'For goodness sake don't fuss! You'll
get your pearls, or some new ones; I'll
see to it myself the moment I get away
from this dreadful hole of a place.'

She leapt to her feet and left the
room, slamming the door behind her.
The noise disturbed Barnaby who
began to cry, and I had to comfort him
and then prepare our meal so there was
little time to think more on the matter.

But that night I had a dream about
Lucas Silver. I dreamed that he was
holding my pearls in his hands,

caressing their smooth loveliness, slipping the milky beads between his long fingers.

'Come to me, Elizabeth,' he said.

Against my will I had to walk towards him until we were almost touching; then his warm hands were on my neck, fumbling with the clasp, and he began stroking my skin.

I awoke in a cold sweat, shivering at the reality of my nightmare.

Dreams of Mr Silver were often to disturb me after that although I had never dreamed about him before. Now, looking back, I know that he took my pearls in order to have something of mine in his possession; whilst I knew nothing of this he could not communicate with me, but once Merry informed me of the fact he was able to reach me in my sleep.

Fortunately I was made of sterner stuff than my sister and during my waking hours he did not disturb me. But once asleep I lost control of my brain and Mr Silver was able to penetrate my sleeping mind.

It was then, after one such nightmare, that I first began to search for a means of escape, a chance to get away and start a new life where Mr Silver could not find me. Merry was too closely bound to the man, she would never leave him, but Barnaby was now my concern. With every new day I realised how much the boy meant to me, and was determined not to hand him over into the clutches of his weird and unnatural father. The thought of the child acting like a puppet, whilst Lucifer pulled the strings, revolted me. Lucas Silver and Merry did not deserve such a son and I made up my mind that they would never take him from me.

In April Merry received the long awaited letter to say that Silver would be coming for her on the following Friday. I dreaded his visit, but decided to see him because I wanted my necklace returned to me.

He came in the afternoon, in Cousin Grace's carriage driven by John, and I allowed Merry to meet him at the door and take him into the parlour for some minutes before I joined them.

Such a fuss she made before he arrived, trying on dress after dress, ripping them off her body, close to tears in her feverish robing and disrobing.

'That green is hideous on me, my skin looks sallow. And the pink is faded, and my best blue velvet is torn!' She dissolved into tears eventually, bright spots of colour staining her cheeks. I knew it was useless to say anything, so I stood by, waiting for her to make up her mind.

'Why are you smiling? It is scarcely a comical matter, and you — you look like an elderly housekeeper in that awful brown serge. Have you nothing more welcoming to put on for his arrival?'

'No.' I folded my hands across my waist and waited composedly.

It was with purpose that my dreariest gown had been chosen, not for anything would I appear to have dressed up, as if this were a special occasion. But when later I met Silver's eyes above Merry's fair head, and saw the mocking expression in them, I realised that he knew exactly my intent and was amused by it.

'Dear sister Elizabeth, may I call you that? For we are more closely linked now than before.' He moved forward to kiss me but I stood rigid, averting my face, as his beard brushed against my cheek. 'Ah, Elizabeth, I hoped that time would have softened your antagonism.'

'Where are my pearls?' I forced myself to look at him. 'I should like them back.'

'They are in my safe keeping.' His eyes glinted as they looked down at my neck, and I felt myself redden, remembering the vividness of my dreams.

'Kindly return them to me, sir. They do not belong to you and I want them.'

'Let us make a bargain, Elizabeth. You may have your pearls when I have my son.'

'What do you mean?'

'I mean that we do not trust each other, perhaps foolishly, and therefore we each hold something precious which belongs to the other. When I come finally to collect my son, I shall bring your necklace with me.'

I hated him; hated the knowledge in his black eyes, the way in which he saw into my heart, knowing how much I cared for Barnaby already.

'Of course there need not be separation in the future,' Mr Silver went on soothingly. 'Once Merry and I can openly claim our child we will just as willingly welcome you into the family. Come also, Elizabeth, there is much you could do to assist me, and I know that we would benefit from your strength and common sense.'

'Lucas, no!' Merry plucked at his sleeve. 'She fusses so — you could never abide that.'

'But I admire a woman with a mind, and a will, of her own. Elizabeth would be an asset,' he said, his eyes on my face.

'Thank you, but I do not enjoy the company of murderers.'

His eyes flashed and I wondered if I was being foolish to so abuse him. But then Silver turned from me and, taking Merry's arm, he went upstairs with her to see his son.

Whilst they were away I took a mug of hot tea out to John, and told him to come in when he had finished and take my sister's belongings out to the carriage.

'How is your mistress?' I asked, before returning to the house. 'Is she well?'

'As well as can be expected, Miss, after all the travellin' she's bin doing. Fair wore out she looked that first day home. But she's better now and will regain her old strength once she's proper rested.'

I nodded and walked thoughtfully back to the front door. Perhaps Lucas Silver could make the old lady sicken, but he would not want her to die until he knew the contents of her will. Would

90

she bequeath him everything? How he must long to know. Maybe, with his strange powers, he did know and thus stayed close to her, showering her with kindness and attention in the hope that she would alter her testament in his favour?

Merry and Mr Silver were in the kitchen when I returned and the magician was holding Barnaby in his arms.

'You should not have brought him down!' I cried, moving swiftly forward to take the baby. 'So much petting is not good for him and he will not be fed for two more hours.'

'The child is mine,' answered Mr Silver softly, 'and I shall do with him what I will.'

My hands fell to my sides. 'Then why all this secrecy? Why do you not take Barnaby with you to London? Why this plotting and concealing, then, Mr Silver?'

'You know very well, Elizabeth, that this is only for the present. Soon things will be different and I shall claim my son.' His eyes burned into mine and I felt helpless, standing as mute as a bashful child before him. 'Never forget that Barnaby belongs to me and one day I shall take him from you. Do not love too greatly, my dear, for I do not wish to see you hurt.'

He looked away from me down at the baby, who was chuckling and trying to grasp the silver medallion around the man's neck. I wanted to cry out, nausea rising in my throat as the baby's little hand grabbed at the shining serpent's head. But I forced myself to turn from the sight for I was unwanted at the family gathering, and without authority so long as Lucas Silver remained with his son.

★ ★ ★

Once Merry had gone back to London I settled to a calm and happy routine; going to the school, returning to housework and cooking and caring for

Barnaby. But everything had a purpose now, I earned money and cleaned and baked for the little boy, and on warm days I allowed him to lie almost naked in the sunshine.

Miss Bloster was not impressed.

'He is as brown as a tinker's child,' she told me tartly. 'You should shield his skin from the sun's rays, Elizabeth, what are you thinking of?'

'Of his health and comfort,' I replied happily, and gloried in Barnaby's firm plump flesh and glowing skin. He ate and he slept and he grew, and I pitied the other babies I saw who were swathed in petticoats and bonnets and remained as white as their crisply starched apparel.

It was a carefree delightful summer, and all the more so after I received a brief note from my sister telling me that they were off on a tour of the continent.

'We are going to Germany and Switzerland,' she wrote, 'where Lucas has a number of engagements. And as Cousin Grace desires to winter in Italy, do not expect to see us again until next year. Lucas says take good care of the child and asks me to tell you that he has not forgotten your pearls.'

I could afford to scorn the man at this distance, and with the knowledge that he was safely abroad again, I dreamed of him only occasionally and then in a muted, dim fashion, as if through a veil of mist. No doubt my peace of mind helped, and my wish for the pearls diminished with the realisation that nothing was as important as the living, laughing, loving child I now possessed. Let Lucifer keep my necklace — I would retain his son.

But how? Over the next few months, as autumn closed in on the land and winter reared its desolate head, I began to think more carefully as to how I could leave town and make it impossible for Lucas Silver to trace me. That he could reach me through my pearls had been proven, but possibly this would not be so easy for him now that my obsession about them was easing?

And what if I left town and went to a place unknown to Silver, could he make contact then? Although not knowing the address, he might still be able to send messages, particularly at night, and could doubtless make my life unpleasant.

But all that was for the future. First I must make my escape and see that Barnaby and I were safely away before Cousin Grace and her party returned to England.

On a cold, crisp December day, shortly before Christmas, I enlisted Miss Bloster's aid. She was an old and trusted friend of Mother's and had proved a kind and understanding employer to me. I knew that such a venture could not be managed on my own, and decided that the old school teacher would be the ideal person from whom to seek advice.

She came to tea on Sunday afternoon, bringing a soft wool ball for Barnaby which she had made herself.

Once I had settled the baby on his

rug with his toys around him, I sat down beside my companion and smoothed back my hair.

'May I speak to you on a very serious matter? I need advice badly and could only think of you.'

'What is it, my child?' She looked at me curiously. 'Of course I shall always help you on any matter. Speak your mind, Elizabeth.'

'Miss Bloster, Merry was not married to this child's father, indeed she is still unwed, and in many ways I am thankful for he is an evil man.'

My companion blinked. 'Am I to understand that you are speaking about Mr Silver? That strange man whom I saw briefly at your father's funeral?'

'The same.' I told her about Lucas Silver's odd life, and the reasons for their not marrying, and the extraordinary powers he had which even reached out to affect me. I did not tell her about his former wife. I had no definite proof about her and besides, the thought of that poor woman was still too painful for me to speak about her with composure. 'I am frightened of Mr Silver,' I went on, 'and of his influence over Barnaby, and do not think that he and Merry will make good parents. No, don't say anything yet,' I added quickly, as Miss Bloster was about to speak, 'tell me only do you believe that I love Barny? Do you think that I can and do care for him sufficiently, and give him the love and attention which every baby should expect from a mother?'

'I do, my dear, you are wonderful with him and I can see that your affection is mutual. But nonetheless, and I must say this, you have no right to him, child. Only the parents have that right.'

'Parents who are not married? Who live a farce? Who are so afraid to face the world with the grubby truth that they hide their child until it suits them to acknowledge his existence? And what of Barnaby's future, Miss Bloster? How will it affect him in later years when he is given to strangers and expected to act like a performing monkey?'

'Elizabeth, calm yourself. Have you not some brandy in the house? I think we could both do with something strong for our nerves.'

'Elderberry wine which I made myself,' I answered tightly.

'That will do nicely. Fetch us some, my dear, and take yourself in hand. I promised to help, if I could, but up till now I do not know what it is you require.'

'A place of refuge.'

I brought out the wine and some glasses, then Barny wanted something to drink so I had to attend to him. But eventually we sat together more calmly, and I was able to continue.

'I want to sell this house and move right away from here, Miss Bloster. Somewhere I can work, for I shall need money, and where I may have the child with me. You have many contacts and much knowledge, can you think of anyone who might help us? All dealings must be accomplished with the utmost secrecy, for Lucas Silver is wily and stubborn and will do his utmost to discover our whereabouts.'

'You must give me time to think,' Miss Bloster replied, sipping thoughtfully at her wine. 'I must decide in my own mind that you are doing the right thing, not only for yourself but also for Barnaby. Then I shall have to determine upon a plan of action. Leave it with me, Elizabeth. We have a short holiday over Christmas and I will tell you what I have decided in the New Year.'

'Do please make haste,' I begged, 'for there is much to arrange and so little time left in which to manage it all.'

'You must be patient, Elizabeth, for Rome was not built in a day,' answered Miss Bloster in her precise voice. 'You are impetuous and over-nervous at present, but I am not sure if we are within the law on such a matter. I must have time in which to consider.'

'There is no need to worry about the law,' I cried. 'Barny is illegitimate and his mother does not want him. She told me so herself, Miss Bloster, can you believe that?'

'I can.' She nodded grimly. 'Meredith was always selfish and frivolous and would make an unsuitable mother. But we have the father's wishes to contend with, and unfortunately, as I have told you before, we live in a man's world.'

'Mr Silver would not dare to bring the law down against me — at least, not whilst Cousin Grace lives. For she knows nothing about him and Merry, so if we act quickly he can do nothing. It is only he, himself, I fear and that is why I must get away before he returns.'

'It is all very difficult and extraordinary,' said Miss Bloster, standing up and smoothing down her skirt. 'However, I shall think the matter over most carefully during the next weeks. Take heart, Elizabeth, for God is on the side of the righteous and I do not believe that He will desert you in your hour of need.'

How could God help me when I never went to church, nor prayed? But

I did have faith in Miss Bloster, and as she put on her hat and wrapped herself in her cloak, my heart lifted and I felt sure that she would take my part in the drama and find the answer to my problem.

5

In February Barnaby had his first birthday, and I invited Miss Bloster and Mrs Stubbs to tea, and Dr Poole promised that he would pop in later if he had a spare minute. Although I had frequently questioned Miss Bloster she still had not come up with a plan of action, and I was beginning to feel that I would never escape from the town.

On the twenty-sixth I awoke early to find that it was a perfect morning with the smell of spring in the air. When Barny was ready for his morning sleep I placed him in the baby carriage out in the garden; he had not lain out since the end of October and I knew that he would enjoy being out of doors and able to watch the clouds and the flight of birds overhead.

After icing his cake, blue and white, with a single red candle, and after cleaning the parlour in readiness for my guests, I went upstairs and glanced out of the window. To my horror I saw a tall, black-robed figure standing over the baby, a silent sentinel of doom.

They were back in England and Merry had not written a word.

I made a rush for the stairs and almost fell in my hurry to get out. Through the kitchen I flew, out into the back garden where Mr Silver's ominous form was bending over the sleeping child.

'Don't touch him!' I shouted, leaping forward. 'What are you doing here and why did you not warn me of your visit? And where is Merry?'

'Gently, Elizabeth, or you will startle him.' Lucas Silver straightened and gazed down at me reprovingly. 'It is my son's birthday and I have brought him a present. As his father, do I not have the right to come?'

I turned away to make sure that Barnaby was all right and saw that he was awake and unfrightened, but around his neck was a monstrous object.

'What is that?' I stared in repulsion at a leather thong which encircled the baby's white neck, attached to which hung a large black bean.

'A talisman, if you like.' Mr Silver shrugged. 'Call it what you will. But he is to wear it always and it will keep him safe. The boy looks well, Elizabeth, and you are to be congratulated, I see that you are fulfilling your task with excellent care.'

'He cannot wear such a monstrosity.' I bent to remove the weird necklet but Silver stopped me.'

'No, Elizabeth.' Startled by his tone I looked up into the magician's face, and his eyes pierced mine so that my senses swam. 'Do not touch that amulet or you will be hurt.'

I blinked and slowly withdrew my hands and clasped them tightly in front of me.

'Where is Merry?' I whispered, trying to speak clearly although my head felt muzzy and my voice was not my own.

'Your sister is not well at present. Nothing to worry about, but she picked up some infection in Italy and that is why we returned earlier than anticipated. However, with Cousin Grace's nursing and all the little comforts of home, she will soon mend. She sends her love,' he added.

'What is wrong with her?'

'A slight fever — lack of appetite. It is nothing, Elizabeth, I would tell you if it were serious.'

I had to believe him. Seeing the man again after so many months of peace had renewed my old fears, and his pagan-like gift to Barny increased my worries. I was determined that the child would not wear that thing around his neck for a moment longer than was necessary. As soon as Mr Silver departed the vile object would be taken off and burnt.

'How did you come here?' I asked, as he remained silent and tension built up between us. 'I did not hear the carriage.'

'On my broomstick.' He smiled and put his hands upon my shoulders, and although I tried to pull away he would not release me. 'Elizabeth, why do you always fight me? There is such rapport between us, and you have great power also, can you not feel it?' He paused and nodded. 'Yes, you are aware of it, and you fear it as you fear me. What a foolish, distrustful girl you are.' He gave me a little shake. 'And passion, can you feel that too?' His eyes wandered to my lips, and I could feel my heart pounding with disgust at the almost physical sensation of his mouth on mine. 'Do not struggle so!' He held me still, his eyes raised to mine again, and I swallowed, trying to look away yet unable to avoid his gaze. 'I could teach you so much if you would but relent and come with me.'

'Never!' I said hoarsely.

'Merry would accept, as she agrees to everything I do,' he went on, 'and your

Cousin Grace likewise. Come with me, you and Barnaby, and we will say that you have adopted him. It would be a fine way out of our predicament, and I will dress you in jewels and splendid finery, and introduce you to the Prince of Wales and watch his face turn green with envy!' He lifted his head and let out a bark of laughter.

'I want you, Elizabeth. Never have I met a female who so enticed me. Have you not heard me calling you in the night?'

His hands were heavy on my shoulders, caressing, rubbing through the material of my dress, and then they slid upwards towards my throat, and his face was the face in my dreams, closing down upon me, blotting out the sky, and his breath was hot against my cheek.

Suddenly a thrush began to sing, loud and clear above our heads in the old apple tree, and so insistent was his call, so clear and lovely, that it called me back to reality and I jerked my head away, avoiding the contact of Lucas Silver's lips on mine.

'Look at me, Elizabeth.'

'No.' Self-possession restored, I looked down upon the green grass thrusting beneath my feet. 'When you have finished mauling me, Mr Silver, perhaps you would remove yourself back to London. You are not wanted here.'

The spell was broken and with a muffled exclamation the man slid his hands off my shoulders and dug them deep into the pockets of his robe. 'You have won this time, my dear, but I will make you a promise, as I did once before, if you remember? I told you that our lives were linked and that has now been proved. Barnaby has forged a bond which nothing can tear asunder.'

I lifted my head and looked back at him scornfully, knowing that my strength had returned.

'You may look like that, disdainful wench!' Silver's voice quickened and I knew that he was angry. 'But one day, my dear, you will come to me and it will not be in such a high-minded fashion. Oh no, Elizabeth, you will come crawling, begging for my love, totally broken in mind and spirit. This I foretell, and you must know by now that I am never wrong.'

My eyes widened and my breath came too quickly for comfort, as I felt my heart thumping painfully against my ribs.

'You may be right, I cannot say. But this I do know. Until such a time as you prophesy, Lucas Silver, I shall fight you and totally reject you and your evil works.'

' 'Get thee behind me, Satan'?' he queried, with a grim smile. 'Brave Elizabeth, how I wish that your sister possessed but a quarter of your courage.' He glanced back at Barnaby. 'Go on caring for my son as you have up till now and I shall be well pleased. There are no other hands that I would so gladly leave him in at present. Au revoir, Elizabeth, till next we meet.'

Before our mid-day meal I carried Barny upstairs into my room and placed him on the floor, then I fetched the largest pair of scissors in my possession and sat on the floor beside the child, explaining what I was going to do.

There did not seem to be any fastening in the leather, so it would have to be cut. How had Silver managed to get it around the boy's neck, for it did not appear wide enough to be forced over his head?

Barnaby watched with large, puzzled eyes and patted the bean with his pudgy fingers.

'Yes, darling, you may still keep it but I do not want it always to be round your neck. You might choke, Barny, or lie on it in the night. It won't be comfortable, sweetheart, so I'm going to cut it away.'

I picked up the scissors but Barnaby crawled away from me, his face puckering.

'Barny, I won't hurt you. Come, let

me hold you, I'll show you what I want to do.'

But he screamed then, in anger, and beat at me with his small fists. He had never turned on me before and, worried about the effect of the bean, and irritated by his childish defiance, I caught his hands in my left one and tried to bring the scissors down on the thong without pricking his skin.

Barnaby was squealing like a little pig and I was sweating with angry exertion, when suddenly a terrible pain streaked up my right hand, high into my arm, and I let scissors and child fall as I folded myself forward over my knees, clutching at my throbbing limb.

I was vaguely aware of Barny crawling swiftly away as I rocked to and fro, trying to soothe the agonising ache in my arm. Gradually it subsided and I was able to lift my head and breathe more freely.

Barnaby sat in the farthest corner of the room, one hand on his bean, the thumb of the other in his mouth.

'Oh, Barny.' I sat and looked at his tear-streaked face and great reproachful eyes, then I held out my arms. 'I'm sorry, darling, that was a silly idea. Look — no scissors, Barny, I won't do that again. Come, darling.'

He stared for a moment, unsure of me, then he gave a muffled sob and crawled forwards. I gathered him up against me, feeling the warm, precious body trembling in my arms.

'Silly, silly, Mama,' I murmured into his curls, comforted by his nearness, yet wondering bleakly how I could ever hope to combat Lucifer's supernatural force.

Of course I could not hide the extraordinary necklet, Barnaby was forever patting it and stroking it, and so I had to make up a tale about his Godfather sending the gift, for Mrs Stubbs' benefit.

'He is an explorer,' I explained that afternoon, 'and travels much in Africa, I believe. I do not care for such heathen decoration but Barny has fallen in love with the wretched thing and refuses to take it off.'

Mrs Stubbs eyed the bean with astonishment but fortunately appeared to believe my story, and Miss Bloster remained tactfully silent although her lips were pressed firmly together in disapproval.

Barnaby spent a happy afternoon, with Dr Poole swinging him between his legs and giving him rides on his bony knees, and we women singing nursery rhymes with the appropriate actions, so that he was right royally entertained.

During the birthday celebrations I was able to forget the hateful bean and Mr Silver's visit for an hour or two, but after Mrs Stubbs and Dr Poole had left, I asked Miss Bloster to stay to supper. Once Barnaby was safely tucked up in bed we sat together in the kitchen and I told the school mistress about that morning's frightening events.

'I cannot remain here a moment longer,' I cried. 'We must get away,

Miss Bloster, we must!'

'I have thought a great deal about what you have told me,' she returned, 'and now with this unpleasant occurrence my mind is quite made up. I do not believe that the boy could be in better hands than yours, Elizabeth, and most certainly not in the hands of that unsuitable man. I am throwing caution to the winds and have already begun plans for you, my child.'

'Thank heavens!' I breathed, sitting forward at the table, my hands clasped beneath my chin. 'Can we leave soon? I could not abide many more days here with the knowledge that Mr Silver might descend upon us again at any moment.'

'A little more patience, Elizabeth, and a satisfactory reply from my sister, and then you will be gone.'

'Your sister? I did not know that you had any family.'

Miss Bloster smiled. 'I have a very dear sister whom I seldom see, unfortunately, as she lives many miles away in Kent. But I think she will aid you — indeed, she seems to be the answer to our prayers.'

Miss Hannah Bloster was house-keeper at Starrling, I was informed, a large farm near Tunbridge Wells, and as she was several years older than my Miss Bloster and wished soon to retire from her post, she hoped that I would take over her job.

'A housekeeper in a large country house? But I have no experience in such matters and am far too young for such a position,' I cried in anguish.

'Hear me out, Elizabeth. Hannah writes that there is little money left, and she and the young master live in three rooms of the manor house. Mr David Starr inherited nothing but debts, apparently, but loves his home and is working desperately hard to build it up to its former prosperity.

'It is a long sad story, but you will doubtless hear all about the family's misfortunes when you go there. Suffice it to say that Hannah cooks for Mr

Starr, does the small amount of cleaning and washing which is necessary for the one man, and longs to retire to the Lodge which her employer has given her for her own.

'It is a very lonely place so you are unlikely to meet any people, and Mr Starr has agreed that you may have your child with you.'

'It sounds ideal!'

'I have told Hannah only that you wish to disappear from this part of the country without trace, and that I vouch for you completely. Mr Starr knows nothing except that you require employment.'

I stretched my hand across the table to clasp one of her thin ones. 'How can I ever thank you enough? A great weight has lifted from my mind and I believe that Barny and I will be safe in such a place.'

'I shall miss you both.' For a moment Miss Bloster's pale eyes were filled with sadness, then she straightened her back and gave her head a little shake. 'This is no time for sentimentality. Now, I wish to buy this house from you, Elizabeth. I know what your dear Papa paid for it and will give you a little extra in addition as I realise that prices have risen these last few years. Also, I do not think your wages will be adequate, for Hannah has been working for next to nothing because she is so fond of her young master. But you have both yourself and Barnaby to care for, so money is essential.

'I have been asked by several parents to open a boarding establishment, and as this house is close to my school it will make a convenient home for the girls who come to stay. I intend paying the money into the bank here for you, and once you are quite settled and need the money near by, I shall make the necessary arrangements with Mr Willard, who, of course, knew your Papa.

'As I shall be taking over here, any letters which are addressed to you will be sent on discreetly, but no one will be told of your whereabouts until, or unless, you wish it.'

'Not even Merry, Miss Bloster — she can be very persuasive, you know.'

'No one,' answered Miss Bloster firmly. 'And I am certain that you will be safe, Elizabeth, for nobody here knows that I have a sister. I do not gossip about my private life,' she added primly.

'But what of Mr Silver? What when he questions you?' I shuddered, thinking of his rage when he discovered that we were gone.

'I shall not lie, Elizabeth. I will simply tell him that my lips are sealed.'

'He might force you to tell — avoid his eyes, I beg you, they can force one to do anything.'

I remembered the elderly lady in London who had feared birds, and the trusting way in which she had looked into Lucas Silver's face, and the way in which his power had entered her mind, conquering her weakness.

'I do not think he will have any

success with me,' answered my companion coldly.

Looking at the frosty expression on Miss Bloster's face, I had to suppress a smile. If Lucas Silver should ever come face to face with the school teacher, he would surely have met his match.

'There is one last point, Elizabeth,' she went on, 'I have told Hannah that your name is Beth Wood and that the boy is called James. Then, if there is gossip amongst the farm folk, or in a neighbouring village, your names will not give you away. Luckily Barnaby is still young enough to accept this change, providing you start right away, so you must school yourself to use those names from now on.'

6

On the tenth day of March, in the year 1881, Beth Wood and her son, James, began their new life at Starrling.

Just after dawn, on a cold misty morning, an open wagon rolled up to our door and Jamie and I were bundled into it, with one small trunk which held my dearest possessions. All the furniture was left behind, all Mother's precious ornaments and trinkets; the cutlery and crockery and linen were abandoned, as were the few rugs and pictures. We were refugees, Jamie and I, leaving everything behind us and starting a new life with little more than the garments we were wearing.

Speed was the essential thing, and light travelling a necessity, for the longer the ramshackle vehicle was standing outside our house, the more likelihood there was of curious neighbours peering out to gossip later about what they had seen.

Miss Bloster spent that last Saturday night with us and after making a hot cup of tea for me, and a bowl of porridge for Barnaby, she had waved us away from the door, a thin, angular lady in a grey dress. Dismally, I had wondered if we would ever see her again.

A surly old man had been sent to escort us to Starrling, and in his grumpy state was an ideal person to accompany us. He spoke not one word the entire journey east, and as Jamie soon fell asleep on my lap, warmly wrapped in a blanket, I was left alone to think my own thoughts, and to ponder on the enormity of what I had done.

Miss Hannah was not at all like her sister, except for the same light coloured eyes and thin-bridged nose. She was large and plump and jolly, a very motherly type of female, but lacked the brains and perception of her younger sister. Her legs troubled her and she moved slowly, obviously thankful to have a younger, nimbler person to hand over to.

Miss Hannah did not move at once to her cottage at the gate, but stayed three days with me in the big house, explaining and chattering and showing me everything that had to be done for her beloved Master David.

'Such a good man,' she told me, that first morning as she was showing me round. 'He works all day long, seven days of the week, yet finds time every Sunday to put on his best suit and walk to church. We have prayers in the kitchen every morning before breakfast — I hope that you are a believer, Mrs Wood? For his religion is very important to Master David.'

I flushed and ducked my chin, momentarily lost for words, and she fortunately took the head movement for a nod, because she beamed her approval and went on with her chatter without waiting for a reply.

Miss Hannah asked me nothing about myself, taking for granted the fact that Jamie was my son, and doubtless, by noticing my ringless fingers, imagined that he was a love child, and that my past was none of her business.

And Mr Starr? He, too, accepted me for what I was, another pair of hands and another pair of legs to run around the desolate shell of his once lovely home. He loved children, obviously, and spent more time talking to Jamie than he did to me.

At first I was not sure what to make of David Starr. He was unlike the other men I had known, lacking Mr Arthur Drew's diffident charm, and Lucas Silver's evil magnetism. My employer was small and thin, white-faced, despite his out-of-door way of life, and fair-haired, which added to his lack of distinction. He also had a pronounced limp, and was so quiet moving and soft-spoken that it was easy to ignore him. He neither repulsed nor attracted me, so it was not difficult to settle into my new surroundings and feel at home there. Certainly, Mr Starr's pious life was bearable, for he did not request me to accompany him to worship on Sundays, and the prayers every morning were short, to my relief.

My wages were low, as Miss Bloster had warned, my employer paying me but ten pounds a year, less than Merry had earned with Mrs Drew. But, in fact, after the sale of my house and the two sovereigns which kind Miss Bloster had pressed into my hand on leaving her, I considered myself to be a woman of some means. And living as we did, with lodging and food all free, I used little of my money save to buy cloth for the few dresses I required, and the necessary garments for Jamie.

My new home was large with ten bedrooms, eight of which had no furnishings, and two with the windows boarded up for lack of glass. There was a narrow gallery which overlooked the hall and through which water seeped on wet days, and the long drawing-room was empty and cold.

We lived all day in the huge kitchen, which was warm and dry, with a stove and an open grate on one side of the room, fed by the great basket of logs which was replenished daily. The kitchen was spacious enough for Jamie to run and tumble in on wet days, and he and I shared the bedroom upstairs which had belonged to Miss Hannah. Mr Starr occupied the only other furnished room which was across the passage from us.

It was sad to see such a home in disrepair, but its owner was determined to restore it, once he had the money. That seemed increasingly unlikely, so far as I could judge, for every penny he made had to be ploughed back into the land. Mr Starr had allowed much of his acreage to become scrubland, and his herd of cows had dwindled to a mere eight. But he refused to give up hope, and would sit for hours in the evenings, with papers and books before him, making calculations and looking so weary that my heart went out to him.

He had no way with women, which suited me, but animals were greatly attracted to him, and he was followed everywhere by a black and white sheep-dog named Jip, and numerous half-wild cats which ran behind him whenever he crossed the yard.

After Miss Hannah left, he asked me if we could have the creatures inside of an evening.

'You do not mind?' he queried, holding the door open for a stream of many-coloured objects which poured into the kitchen. 'Hannah would not allow them in but they are quite clean and love the warmth. I do not wish to throw them out, unless you object?'

'I do not mind,' I answered. It was his house and they were inside by then, anyway.

So the cats came to stay and spent every evening by the fire after that. Jamie, too, loved the creatures and would sit for ages, staring into the flames with an arm around one, a small hand lovingly caressing the back of another.

My work was enjoyable, and although vigorous it was not difficult. Mr Starr always rose first in the mornings and went down to the kitchen, where he built up the fire so it was nice and warm for my descent, put on the kettle, and washed in the sink. Then he took a piece of bread and dripping from the larder and went out for the morning's milking.

At first it troubled me that he had to do so much himself, but Miss Hannah assured me that this was his way, and that he liked being on his own early in the day. She, certainly, never stirred herself until he left the house, so it did not seem right for me to do so.

The clanking of buckets and churns from the dairy awakened me, and in a leisurely fashion I would wash myself and Jamie, in the basin of water which I kept in our room, and then we would dress and go downstairs to prepare the breakfast which Mr Starr came in for at about seven-thirty. With my employer came the Gritt family, and as they also took their mid-day meal with us, I was kept busy cooking and washing-up for six people.

Samuel Gritt was the surly carter who had fetched us, and his wife, Miriam, was equally close-mouthed, and assisted at milking and in the fields. Their son, Job, was a big, strong lad but he was simple-minded, so that conversation around the table was far from exciting. Mr Starr was frequently lost in thought and as our other three companions did not utter, I was left to converse with Jamie. It was a relief when the chairs scraped back, grace was said, and everybody removed themselves for the day's labour.

Job was a kind, well-meaning fellow, who smiled readily, but I could not make out a word he said. He grew very fond of Jamie and would often take him round the barns and outbuildings, showing him the young calves, and the secret places where the mother cat had hidden her kittens.

I would not trust him with the child further afield, although Mr Starr assured me that he was a reliable lad, but as long as they remained within sight and sound of the kitchen I allowed Jamie this freedom.

Once I was used to my new routine and had worked out a time-table for myself, I intended tackling all the rooms in the house. They were in a dreadful state when I arrived, for Miss Hannah had had neither the strength nor the time for such unnecessary chores. But I felt that although they were deserted, they could be swept and dusted occasionally, and the floors, of good wood, would respond beautifully to a vigorous polish.

It was a busy life, but a happy one, and I revelled in the sense of security which the isolated farm gave to me. The cooking and the stores had to be carefully managed, for there were no shops near by and Mr Starr went into town but once a week for provisions. I had the chickens to tend and would go out twice a day with Jamie to collect the eggs and then wash them ready for market.

I also began working in the vegetable garden behind the house. It was overgrown and hopelessly neglected, for no one had had the time to cultivate it, but I intended spending a few hours there each day. It had once been a fine source of supply, for the beds were carefully laid out and there was an abundance of fruit bushes, all tangled now and in dire need of pruning. But no vegetables were grown there and I was determined to do my part in putting that right.

Jamie and I also visited Miss Hannah each week; it made a pleasant walk down the long drive to her cottage at the gate, and she had made a comfortable home for herself. It was in good repair, to my surprise, but apparently Mr Starr and Samuel had worked every spare minute to make it habitable again. I wished that the men could spare some time for the big house, but that had to wait; every minute was important on the land with summer just round the corner.

I began wearing breeches two weeks after settling at Starrling. It was a good thing that we had no near neighbours for it was most unseemly for me to stride about in male garb. But Mr Starr did not object to my wearing them and with a pair of my employer's cast-offs covering my lower limbs, and a pair of his boots swamping my feet, I could tramp through mud and briars without a care. It was sensible attire for the garden, after all, where skirts and petticoats would only have hindered my work.

Mr Starr would sometimes pass by and take the spade from me, frowning at my perspiring form.

'That is not the work for you, Mrs Wood,' he would say gruffly, 'ask Miriam, to give you a hand with the heavy stuff, you cannot manage alone.'

But I liked the feeling of the wooden spade in my hands, and the satisfaction of seeing square after square turned and ready for seed, and I did not desire the sharp-faced woman's company. She looked askance at me every time I appeared in breeches, and made it obvious that my presence at Starrling was resented. Had she hoped for the position of housekeeper once Miss Hannah retired? Though with her slatternly appearance and miserable countenance, I doubted that Mr Starr would have considered her; not that my appearance was much better, but at least I kept myself clean and always changed into a gown for the evenings.

My employer was the easist man in the world to care for; eating whatever was set before him, always grateful for whatever I did. I appreciated him all the more when remembering Father's irritability and Merry's selfish moods. He was a restful and quiet companion in the evenings, and read a good deal in the sagging chair beside the hearth.

Once Jamie was tucked up in bed I would join Mr Starr with my sewing, sitting across from him, darning and mending his clothes which were pitifully threadbare.

It was the only time which we had to ourselves, for then Samuel and his family went home for the night and Mr Starr and I could relax. Sometimes we played cribbage, a card game which he taught me, and at other times he would read aloud, verses of poetry which he particularly admired, and his voice was pleasant and soothing.

'How did Starrling come to be in such a sorry state?' I asked him, a few weeks after Miss Hannah had departed, feeling that we knew each other well enough by then and that he would not find my question impertinent. 'May I ask you that?'

'Of course.' Mr Starr put down his book and smiled across at me. 'I was wondering when we would get beyond the 'Good morning' and 'Good night' stage, Mrs Wood.'

'Miss Hannah said that I was not to bother you with questions for you were weary of an evening and did not care for foolish chatter.'

'Hannah, bless her, could only chatter, but I have nothing against a reasonable conversation. Can you converse, Mrs Wood?'

'I can try, sir. Please tell me about this house. How did your family come to lose all its money? This was a beautiful home once.'

'Call me David,' he said. 'I have no mind for formalities. Yes, once this was beautiful. Once upon a time there was a farmer living here, a simple, good-natured fellow, by the name of Matthew Starr, who worked his land well and was satisfied with his acreage and pleasant way of life.'

My employer stretched out his feet towards the fire. 'He owned five hundred acres of good arable land, had six diligent men working for him, and he cared for them and their families and was content with his small but comfortable home.

'Then one day he met a Miss Charlotte Ling, who was visiting with relations in Tunbridge Wells, and he fell in love with her. She came from Bedfordshire and possessed a fortune, and her head was turned by the tall, handsome farmer from Kent. Soon they married, and out of love and gratitude for all that she had brought into his family, he renamed this place Starrling.'

'A pretty name,' I remarked.

'The young couple were very happy and the farmer used up a great deal of his wife's money making his humble abode worthy of her. That new wing at the west was added, the drive was widened and improved, and more servants were brought into the house. They led a gay and sociable life, for the farmer would do anything to please his Charlotte, but eventually his work suffered from so many late nights and jaunts to London, so a bailiff was employed.

'During the next few years the couple

were blessed with two fine sons, Randolph and Hugo. Both were handsome and well-built like their father, but differed greatly in temperament. Randolph was serious and industrious and grew up to love his father's land, but Hugo became too fond of gambling and women to be of any assistance at home. He spent most of his time in London, squandering every penny, and often more, of his allowance.'

'Was not his father angry?'

'Hugo was his mother's favourite, and to keep her happy the father continued to pay his son's debts, hoping, I have no doubt, that he would grow wiser as he grew older.'

'But he did not?'

'No.'

'And what of David, the third son? You have not mentioned him.'

'David was the runt.'

I glanced up quickly at the bitter tone in his voice, but he did not notice my look and went on staring into the fire.

'David was born many years after

Hugo, ten to be exact, when his mother believed her family to be complete and had no desire for another baby in the house. He was also pale and sickly and cried a great deal, so I have been informed. He was not wanted by anyone in the household, save for the kindly housekeeper.'

'Miss Hannah?'

Mr Starr nodded. 'Hannah, who has been my life-long friend, and whom I shall care for as long as we both have breath in our bodies. Nurse-maids, governesses and tutors all came and went, but Hannah remained, a staunch and loving ally.'

'Were you born with — ' I hesitated. 'I beg your pardon, now I am being inquisitive and Miss Hannah would not like it.'

'Hannah is not here and I have to face up to such things. Yes, Mrs Wood, I was born with this twisted limb and at one time nobody thought that I would be able to walk.' He looked down at his leg and ran one hand gently down it to the knee. 'But I did, and it has served me well although I am slow and particularly awkward in damp weather.'

'Poor little boy,' I murmured, imagining Jamie in a crippled state, unable to run or tumble about on the grass as he so loved to do.

'It was not too bad. Fortunately we had money at that time and plenty of servants to aid me. I also loved reading so lying quietly was not too great a burden. But I hated to disappoint my mother, for I loved her dearly, Mrs Wood, and she had no time for me. My father was kind and patient with my slowness, but Mother was lively and easily impatient, needing action and entertainment all day long.' He smiled. 'She was the prettiest creature — I have a picture of her upstairs.'

He went up to his room and returned some while later holding a miniature in his hands. 'Something Hugo did not sell,' he said, holding it out to me.

It was exquisitely painted in a little gold frame, and I looked for a long time at the face, which reminded me of Merry's. A pointed chin, large blue eyes, dainty nose, and the whole crowned by thick golden hair which cascaded in curls and ringlets to her shoulders; a sweet, enchanting, wilful little face.

'You have a look of her about the eyes,' I said, handing the portrait back to its owner.

'I was the most like her. My brothers took after Father who was tall, big-boned and dark. But she did not care for fair men, they looked so weak, she said. I never had the chance to be anything else, but this all came to me in the end.' Mr Starr looked around the kitchen and smiled, somewhat bleakly. 'This became my inheritance once everything was gone,' he said.

'For how long has it been yours? And when did it start declining?'

I imagined the hustle and bustle of the big house as it once was; the servants busy in the kitchen preparing splendid meals for the family and guests; the drive, now pot-holed and laced with weeds, once a-clutter with carriages; and horses and grooms filling the stables, which were now derelict and inhabited by one old horse and many chickens, which scratched and pecked amongst the sacks and cobwebs.

The big hall would have been ideal for dances and parties, with musicians tucked away in the gallery above, and the overflow of guests spilling out into the long drawing-room and, in fine weather, moving further out through the glass doors on to the terrace.

There was a wide fire-place in the drawing-room still, but not a stick of furniture, nor carpets or paintings; shutters had been pulled across the glass doors, and blinds hid all the windows. Upstairs, there was a four-poster bed in what must have been the master bedroom, but apart from our two rooms, all the others were empty.

'My parents both died of the typhoid in 1870,' went on Mr Starr quietly, 'and then Randolph took over here and made a good job of things. But he had two difficulties; Hugo went on spending money recklessly, and though Father had left him a fair portion of money this ran out in three years and Randolph was forced to pay his debts. And secondly, labour was becoming scarce as men sought work in the towns where wages were higher. The bailiff left, as did all our other families, apart from the Gritts. Randolph tried to sell land but nobody wanted it, and from then on Starrling began to go downhill.'

He sighed and passed a hand wearily over his face. 'I watched it all happen and it sickened me, but what could I do save work out there beside Randolph and Samuel Gritt? Watching and learning and listening, serving an apprenticeship which was to stand me in good stead. Then, in January '77, disaster struck again and Randolph broke his neck out hunting.'

'Oh, David!'

'Hugo took over, for my elder brother was completely paralysed and I wish to

God that he had died then. But he lingered for another nine months, Mrs Wood, and I had to witness Hugo selling this home, piece by piece, about our very ears. He would not work in the fields for he bore no love for the land, and the moment he needed more money something of value went from the house.

'I do not think that Randolph knew what was going on, he had the end bedroom and was kept very quiet, but it was upsetting for me and once again I could do nothing.'

'Why did not Hugo sell the entire estate at once and have done with it?'

My employer looked across at me and smiled. 'Would you have had my home taken from me as well as everything else?' he asked gently.

'I did not mean that! I only wondered that he left anything at all — I cannot understand *him*, that is all.'

'Hugo realised that as long as we owned Starrling there was always something more he could sell, if need be, and what would he have done with Randolph? I did not matter, but Randolph was still nominally in control and I do not believe the entire farm could have been disposed of without his signature. It was the books and the paintings and the furniture which went. Anyway,' he leaned forward and took the scrawny tabby cat up on to his knee, 'he did unbelievable harm but only outlived Randolph by a month, fortunately for me.'

'Did somebody shoot him?' I asked hopefully.

'No.' A glint of amusement lightened my companion's eyes. 'Simply a heavy cold which turned into pneumonia and finished him off.'

'Good. And now you will build this place up and make it beautiful again. I am sure you can do it. After so much bad luck your fortunes are certain to change.'

'Thank you for your optimism, but after a series of bad harvests and now the development of the American prairies into fertile grain land, I rather think that agriculture in this country has had its day.'

'You must not say that, nor give in to misfortune! I will help you, if you will let me? I am young and strong and have worked hard all my life. We'll make it work, and this house will lift its head again, I know it will.'

'Then we had better get some sleep.' Mr Starr stood up and tucked the tabby under his arm. 'Out you go, puss, and tackle some of those mice which are causing havoc in the barn. And you others, too.' He hustled the lazy creatures out of the back door with some gentle aid from his foot, then moved back to build up the fire for the night.

'Your encouragement is heart-warming, Mrs Wood, and I admire your efforts in the vegetable garden, but a miracle is necessary if I am ever to put Starrling back on its feet again.'

'We shall see.' I stood up and folded away my sewing. 'In the summer I intend coming out into the fields and helping you. Miss Hannah says you are always desperate for extra help then, and my arms are strong. Good night, David, and pleasant dreams.'

I was so happy that night, filled with enthusiasm at the knowledge that here I was needed, here was a place for me in the company of a man whom I liked and respected, and, moreover, Jamie and I were safely hidden from the world and particularly from the sombre and magnetic eyes of Lucas Silver.

With a little stab of apprehension, I remembered him and his dark Satanic face, and wondered how he and Merry fared. No word had come as yet from Miss Bloster and I had managed to forget the man for days on end. But I could not imagine that he would accept our disappearance with resignation, and wondered what he would do when he discovered that we were gone.

However, at the moment I was certain that Silver was still in ignorance of my escape and so I put memories of him to the back of my mind. Starrling was all that mattered now and was something which would become increasingly dear to me as time went by.

7

That first summer at Starrling passed happily and peacefully, except for one upsetting event.

The trouble occurred when the days became warmer and the sun lit up the green Kentish countryside. I had always made sure that Jamie's necklet lay beneath his clothes, tucked down so that it was concealed by his shirt. But as the days grew warmer he needed less apparel, and on a particularly hot day in August I allowed him to run around with his top half quite bare.

We had been in the vegetable garden all morning and when I went inside to prepare the mid-day meal, I left Jamie playing outside with the kittens in the yard. He wore a frilled sun bonnet so I was not afraid of the heat upon him, and it gave me time alone in the kitchen as I was already late in starting cooking.

At around noon I heard an extraordinary noise and before I could go out and discover what was happening, Job rushed through the door and slammed it behind him, gibbering and gesticulating in a crazed manner. Even when he spoke normally I found it difficult to understand him, but in his present state he was incomprehensible.

'What is it, Job? Whatever is the matter?' I went to him quickly. 'Sit down and rest awhile, you have had a shock.'

He jabbered something at me, his eyes rolling with terror, his great red fist pointing dramatically at the door.

'Yes, I will go and look. Now sit down and calm yourself.'

I took him by the arm, concealing my distaste at touching him for he was an ugly, loutish fellow, with a pock-marked face, whom I found repulsive now, smelling strongly of sweat and with his hair full of corn husks and his skin engrimed with dust.

But Job pulled away from my grasp

and went on pointing at the door in an agitated manner.

Cautiously I went to peer outside, hoping that David would soon arrive. A half-demented man of Job's size was more than I could cope with, and if something had frightened him it seemed unlikely that I should be able to tackle it.

But outside all was calm in the noon-day heat; a few chickens pecked their way across the yard, the dust shimmered in front of my anxious eyes, and there was nothing else moving save for Jamie, who sat with a kitten on his lap, patting at the earth with his fat hands.

Job let out another hoarse yell behind me and pointed at the child with a shaking finger.

'It's only Jamie,' I said, moving forward. 'Are you all right, love? Perhaps you had better come out of the sun now. Maybe Job means it is too hot for you?' I walked across to him and stretched out my hand. 'Come on in, darling, it is almost time to eat.'

Jamie rose and clutched my fingers, but as we turned back to the open doorway, Job yelled again and with a bull-like rush, lowered his head and fled across the yard, bawling at the top of his voice.

I looked down at Jamie in amazement and then I saw it — the bean necklace — so obvious on his little naked chest.

Oh no, I thought wearily, he's not making all the fuss about that, surely?

But he was, and he brought Samuel and Miriam running, and David, more slowly with his bad leg, bringing up the rear. All three wore worried expressions and as I gathered Jamie up into my arms and faced the onrush, Samuel and Miriam stopped before me, panting and cross, as if I had alarmed their son.

'I do not know what has upset Job,' I began, 'he seems frantic about something.'

'What the devil is going on?' asked David, slowing to a walk as he came across to join us. 'Are you all right, Mrs

Wood? And the boy?'

'We are both fine,' I said, 'but something is worrying Job. I rather think it might be this silly thing which Jamie is wearing. Job hasn't seen it before because it is usually tucked away beneath his shirt. Do assure the lad that it is only an African bean which Jamie's Godfather sent for his birthday. I cannot communicate with him at all.'

'How can that have upset him?' asked David in astonishment. 'Job, here, lad. Come and tell us what troubles you.'

Job skulked round the corner of the barn and inched his way towards us, rubbing the back of his hand across his face.

'He don't seem happy,' muttered his mother, glaring at me. 'Seems like someone's upset him.'

'I have already told you what it is,' I retorted sharply. 'Kindly come in now before your food gets cold.'

'Funny heathenish lookin' thing to hang around the neck of a babe,' she went on, her black eyes darting to

Jamie's throat. 'Looks proper evil to me, and Job knows — he's got an extra sense to make up for his lack of tongue,' she said.

It was the longest speech Miriam had ever made in my hearing.

'Tell him it is nothing to worry about,' I told her curtly, 'and I will make sure that Jamie always wears a shirt over it in future, so Job will not see it again.'

'Ah, but he'll know it's there, won't he?' she went on in a maddening whine. 'He don't forget nothing, our Job don't.'

I threw an exasperated glance at David, then turned on my heel and carried the child into the kitchen.

'Stupid, ignorant people with their silly superstitions,' I muttered to Jamie, pulling off his sun bonnet and tugging a shirt over his head. 'There — wear that for now, darling, and we'll get your clothes off you the moment those peasants go back to the fields.'

I heard David talking outside in the

yard but could not make out what he was saying. Some few minutes later they all trooped into the kitchen, but Job refused to sit in his usual place beside Jamie and settled himself instead on the far side of David. The meal was uncomfortably silent, with all three Gritts throwing me sullen glances from over the tops of their bowls, as if I were a witch and Jamie, my familiar.

David was quiet, as usual, and once the unattractive family had departed, I turned on him angrily.

'Do they have to eat with us in future? Their manners are appalling and their presence revolts me. And you do not say so much as a word. Could you not try to converse? It may be beyond the Gritt's capacity but it is not beyond mine!'

'Now, now, Mrs Wood, you are frightened and annoyed and I do not blame you, but it is not fair to vent your wrath on the Gritts. They have had a hard life with all their healthy children dying of the small pox, and only poor

Job remaining alive. You must make allowances for them, and the lad was scared almost out of the few wits he does possess. 'Tis a pity, for he was fond of Jamie, here.' He put out a hand and fondled the boy's curls. 'You must admit that that is a most outlandish decoration. Who is this Godfather, Mrs Wood?'

'That is none of your business,' I snapped, 'and why anyone should be scared of a child's ornament, I do not know.'

'Scarcely a normal trinket. I believe there is more to it than you would have us believe. However,' my employer stood up, putting his chair neatly against the table, 'I shall not question you further as you do not care for my prying. One day, though, I hope you will have enough trust to tell me more about your own and Jamie's past.'

'We have no past.' I began clearing away the dirty dishes. 'Do go out so that I can clear away in peace.'

He smiled and touched my shoulder

154

lightly as he went by. 'Clear away in peace then, and go and rest. You work too hard, my dear, and will wear yourself out if you do not take care.'

'I am quite strong and can work as hard as anyone else if only people would leave me be and not pester so!'

No more was said on the subject of Jamie's bean, but meal times became increasingly awkward and Job continued to keep well away from the little boy. Jamie was puzzled by this attitude for he was fond of 'Jo-Jo' and could not understand the fellow's withdrawal. I tried to explain that Job was not feeling well and we should leave him alone for the present.

I dug Jamie a little patch of his own in the garden, where he played about with a bucket and trowel, and we visited Miss Hannah more often. She felt the heat badly, poor dear, and did not venture out of her cottage during the long hot days. She enjoyed our frequent visits and Jamie was kept occupied and had little time to fret over Job's strange behaviour.

I did not go out to help with the harvest that year, feeling that it was better to keep myself and my son out of sight as much as was possible, but meal times could not be avoided, for David refused me permission to eat earlier with the child, as I had hoped.

'We are like a family,' he told me, 'and as such, we take our breakfasts and lunches together. You must support me in this, Mrs Wood, for the Gritts are all the labour I have left and without them Starrling would truly fall. So hide your disgust, please, and I shall endeavour to be a more lively companion. Then at least outwardly we will make a show of relaxed well-being. I feel sure that Job will quickly forget his fears, he is a simple fellow and time will heal his fright.'

I was not so sure of this, for whenever Job was within sight of Jamie, his eyes would fix themselves upon the bulge beneath the child's shirt. As his mother had predicted, Job knew that the

156

necklet was there, and he would never forget.

However, summer turned to autumn, and winter followed without further mishap, and we jogged along amicably enough, an oddly assorted company in the ramshackle mansion.

Then it was Christmas, with all the excitement and bustle of preparation, and for me it was an especially happy occasion for now my son was old enough to appreciate the festive season, and we had invited Miss Hannah to come up and spend Christmas Day in the big house.

The Gritts, to my delight, were to have the whole day off from work, so our rejoicing would not be marred by their gloomy presence. But David asked me to cook a goose on Christmas Eve so that the family could have a share of our fare.

Once the milking was finished on the twenty-fourth and I had put Jamie to bed, David brought in a fir tree which he had chopped down, and we decorated it together in one corner of the kitchen. Then we filled Jamie's stocking with sweetmeats and nuts, and I tiptoed upstairs to hang it at the foot of his cot.

Later, David and I sipped elderberry wine, which I had made that autumn, and he thanked me for the work I had done over the past months.

'Life has not been easy for you, Mrs Wood, with Job's unaccountable behaviour and the antagonism of his parents. But you have borne these difficulties bravely and I commend you. Working in this desolate house can also not have been easy, and your labours in the vegetable garden have been most welcome. Thank you, my dear, for taking Hannah's place so happily and efficiently. May the New Year bring you nothing but health and good fortune.'

'Thank you kindly, sir,' I answered with a smile, grateful for the praise. Although he was kind and easy to live with, compliments did not often come from my employer, and I appreciated the fact that he had noticed my efforts. Keeping the rooms clean and doing the cooking and gardening had not been difficult, but holding my tongue so far as the Gritts were concerned had been hard at times, as had been the artificial gaiety with which I had presided at communal meal times.

I went to bed early that night, warmed by the wine and David Starr's thoughtful words, and I wrapped his present carefully before getting into bed. It was a pair of woollen socks which I had knitted whenever he was out of the kitchen. His own were so worn and well-darned that a new pair would surely make a pleasant surprise. For Miss Hannah I had the little garnet brooch which had belonged to Mother, and was one of the few things which I had brought with me from home.

Jamie was to have a Noah's Ark. David had unearthed his old playthings from one of the attics, and with some new paint and varnish the animals and boat looked as good as new. This was to be a present from us both, and the toy had been left beneath the tree to wait until morning.

That night my tranquillity ended.

I dreamed a terrible dream and awoke screaming, to find David's arm around my shoulders, his face eerily shadowed by the candle beside my bed.

'Hush, Beth, you are safe now. Hush, or you will frighten Jamie.'

As I sat up, shivering and covered with sweat, I saw Jamie's little white face peering at me from his cot across the room.

'Oh, God!' I covered my face with my hands and burst into tears.

Silver knew. He had discovered that we were no longer at home and he was mad with rage. He had come into my room at Starrling, quite clearly I had seen him standing in his black robe, his eyes flashing above the darkness of his beard.

'Elizabeth.' He had called my name so insistently that I had awakened and sat up to look at him. 'Elizabeth, I have brought you back your pearls,' he said, and soundlessly he had moved towards me, his hands outstretched, and between his fingers I had seen the shimmer of my necklace.

'I don't want them.' I knew that they were linked with Jamie, that if I accepted them Silver would take the child and I would never see him again. I tried to get up, to flee from his approach, but my limbs were numb and I could only sit trapped, sickened with terror by his presence.

'You are a naughty girl, Elizabeth, for running away with my son.' Silver's voice was low, but nonetheless terrifying. 'And you must be punished, for nobody defies me — you must understand that.'

He came right up to the bed and then his hands were round my throat and he was fastening the pearls. Suddenly they were moving; the pearls were disintegrating and reforming, becoming a slithering, writhing coil around my neck and I put up a hand, half-choking, and felt the smooth sinuous body of a snake.

I screamed, screamed aloud in an agony of horror and as Lucifer's laughter faded I awoke properly to hear my own cries, and the voice of David Starr reassuring me.

'It is all right, Beth. You are safe now. No one can harm you.' His arm was warm round my shoulders and I could feel the protecting strength of his body pressed to mine.

'Has it gone? The snake — round my neck — is it there?'

I spoke through my fingers, knowing that there was nothing, that it had all been a gruesome nightmare, yet needing someone to soothe me, to confirm that all my fears were groundless.

'There is nothing, nothing round your neck. Here, give me your hand and feel for yourself.'

David took my fingers and placed them on my throat and round the back beneath my hair, and I felt my bare skin and the ruffled edge of my nightgown. I relaxed against him then, as my breath came more easily and fear subsided.

'It was horrible, horrible,' I whispered, turning my face into his chest. 'He has discovered that we are gone and he will not rest until he finds us. Oh, dear heavens, what am I going to do?'

'You are safe here, Beth. No harm can come to you at Starrling, I promise.'

'But he will find out — he will torment me in my dreams — ' I broke off, seeing Jamie's little white figure in the corner bed, and David's puzzled stare. 'I'm sorry, it was a dreadful nightmare and I am not yet fully recovered. Please leave the candle, David, I cannot sleep without a light.'

'You will be all right now?' he queried. 'Or shall I bring my bedding and lie here on the floor for the rest of the night?'

'Thank you, no, all is well. Go back to bed — you must be frozen. I am sorry for the trouble I've caused.' I managed a shaky smile. 'It must have been too much good food.'

David rose and went across to Jamie and laid him down and tucked him in. 'Go to sleep and I'll see you in the morning. Mama has had a nasty dream but she is calm now and I'll leave the candle for you both.' Then he looked back at me, still crouched in a huddle at the top of my bed. 'You, too, Beth. Lie down and sleep. I had better fetch a night light for that candle will not last till dawn.'

When we were both settled with the night light between us on the table, David took the candle and went back to his own room. Heaven knows if he managed to sleep the rest of that long night, for I did not, and had hours in plenty to dwell upon Lucas Silver and his fantastic powers, and the worry of how we were to continue living peacefully at Starrling now that Lucifer had discovered us.

Christmas Day, to which I had looked forward with a light and happy heart, proved to be the longest sixteen hours of my life, and I dragged myself through them trying to be gay yet feeling like a death's head.

I walked with Jamie down to the cottage and escorted Miss Hannah back to the house, and her voluble chatter helped me a little, as did David's present of golden rings for my ears, and Miss Hannah's pretty scarlet scarf.

We opened all our presents and joked and laughed, and ate well, but by the time that David accompanied Miss Hannah home and Jamie was in bed, my head was splitting with tension, and I sank down at the kitchen table and wept. Great racking sobs which I could not control shook my body, as I was overcome by a terrible dread. There was no way out of this predicament; every waking moment my mind would be filled with thoughts of Lucas Silver, and every night I would have to fight against sleep for fear of what was to come.

Lucifer would never leave me alone

now; every ounce of strength which he possessed would be exerted towards me until he had tormented me beyond sanity, and I would be powerless against his demands.

He wanted his son — my son! And he would come and take him in the end; to control him as he controlled Merry, to manipulate him and ruin his mind, so that my Jamie would become nothing better than a puppet on a string, answering only to his master.

'Beth, no.' David came back into the kitchen and moved towards me, stretching out his hand to touch my bowed shoulders. 'Don't my dear, I cannot bear to see you so.' He sat beside me and took my hands in his and began stroking and rubbing my tensed fingers. 'Tell me about it,' he said softly, 'you must talk now, too much has happened for you to remain silent any longer.'

'I don't know what to do.' Wearily I lifted my head and looked up into his white, strained face. The day must have been an ordeal for him, too, I realised, for he had known that I was under great stress, and had been unable to speak of the matter until now. 'You are most kind but there is nothing anyone can do to help me.'

'We shall see about that. Talk first, Beth, that will ease you. Then we can perhaps make decisions. This man of whom you are so afraid — is he Jamie's Godfather?'

'No. And his name is not Jamie, nor is mine Beth Wood.'

I told him everything then, sitting by the fire that strange Christmas night; I told David all about Merry and Lucas Silver, and Miss Bloster's help in the flight from my home town. It gave me a certain sense of release, unburdening myself onto another person, and some of my tension lifted as I was able to speak freely of the worries which had been locked within my heart for months.

'So you see,' I ended, 'Silver has the whip-hand and I shall be forced to give in to him finally, for without sleep my courage will weaken and without that I stand no chance at all.'

David stood up to place another log on the fire. 'I find this so hard to believe,' he remarked slowly, reseating himself beside me. 'Yet Job's fear was very real, which makes me think there must be something supernatural about the bean. And you, Beth, for I cannot call you by your other name, you are too sensible and downright a girl to have made up such a tale.'

He looked at me for a moment in silence and then a half-smile crossed his face and he returned his attention to the fire.

'Is there something amusing about the situation?' I asked shortly.

'No, but there is a way out. At least, it might help you if you were willing to try.'

I stared. 'What on earth can be done against such an evil force?'

'You could marry me.'

I was so stunned by this reply that words would not come and I sat gaping like some witless fool.

'I am sorry to have shocked you but it seems a reasonable enough plan to me,' he said quietly.

'But — but I had never thought of such an idea!'

'That is obvious.'

'And I do not love you.'

'That is not important.'

'And how could such a proposition possibly help me against Lucas Silver?'

'If you married me, Beth, you would no longer be alone. There would be two of us fighting this man, and although my body is not all that it should be, my faith is strong and I believe God would help us.'

'God? He has never helped me before — why should He start now?'

'Have you ever asked Him?'

I shook my head. 'I need much more than that,' I said impatiently, 'you do not know what this man is like. He is Lucifer, himself. I need something powerful and wholly indestructible to withstand him.'

'Love can be all of those things, Beth; and faith, too, if one has enough.'

'But I have neither, don't you understand?' I stood up and began pacing the kitchen floor, my hands plucking at the folds of my skirt.

'Beth, listen to me.' David swung round from the table, his voice firm as he watched me. 'As your husband I would be with you in the night, to hold and comfort you in your distress. Together we could banish this Silver fellow, and you would never be alone. Jamie could be ours, he could take my name and come under my protection. Do you not see? We would be a proper family then, united in our love and mutual affection.'

'I could not love you.'

It was not meant to sound so harsh but the words had to be said. David Starr was a kind man and I admired his gentleness, but there lay the trouble. I was too strong a personality for such as he, and would too easily override his meekness. A husband must always be master in his house, and David, like Arthur Drew, was not the right man for me.

With a sickening feeling of dread I remembered Lucas Silver's eyes, and the subdued power of his voice, knowing deep within me that what he had foretold would come true. He was the man to master me, fight him though I must, and one day he would lay claim to me and Jamie and we would succumb to his will.

'I am sorry,' I whispered, looking at the slender, pale-faced man at the table, 'but I cannot marry you.'

'It would be a marriage of convenience, Beth, no more than that. I should expect nothing from you save the friendship and companionship which we now share. Is that too much to ask?'

Such humility. He had no idea of Lucifer's power, nor of the hold which he had over me even at this distance. I shivered, shaking my head at the futility of his suggestion, walking up and down, up and down the flagged floor. I willed my brain to envisage a plan which would free me momentarily from the magician's mental torment.

It was all right now, in the warm bright room, with David sitting nearby and with the homely smells of spices and burning wood and damp dog to reassure me. But at night it would be different, lying alone in the darkness, with only Jamie's curled defenceless shape in the corner for company. Then I would know real fear again and would have to fight with all my might; for fight him I must. There would be no easy victory for Lucas Silver, on that I was determined.

Maybe there was a way. A sudden thought struck me and I paused, biting at the fingers of my right hand.

'Dare I ask what passes through your mind?' David's voice broke into my thoughts and I saw that he was still sitting watching me.

'You may ask but you will not receive an answer!' I spun across to bestir the cats, and put my chair to one side of the hearth. 'I think I know what to do. Hurry up, David, to bed! It is almost midnight and you have to be up early on the morrow.'

He looked at me intently, a slight frown on his face. But I whisked past him to open the door and usher out the cats. Jip, I know not why, was allowed to remain inside for the night.

'Out you go, pussies, and good hunting! Now, David, off you go and I'll follow in a moment.'

'Beth.' He stood up but did not move towards the door. 'Beth, I wish you would tell me what you have in mind. It is nothing stupid, is it?'

'Of course not, Mr Starr. How could you imagine such a thing! Sensible, downright females such as I do not behave stupidly.' I smiled and gave him a push towards the door. 'Off with you now, or the poor cows will be fairly bellowing by morning!'

He went out shaking his head, but at least he went, and I was left alone.

Elderberry wine, that was the answer, and the sloe gin also, if there was enough left. I ran to the larder and counted the bottles which had been prepared during the autumn. Nine bottles of wine, and three of the gin not yet opened. I would be saved for many a night and perhaps, if Silver found that he was getting no reaction, he would leave me alone after that.

Taking a bottle of wine and a glass, and hiding them in the folds of my skirt in case David should still be about upstairs, I crept to my room without seeing him and placed my treasures beside my bed. They would do the trick. I knew the potency of that wine, that after three glasses I would be agreeably muzzy-headed, so that if I could down half-a-dozen tonight they would provide the oblivion I sought.

It was difficult swallowing the fourth glassful, sitting up in bed, dribbling it down my chin, beginning to giggle at the sight I must look with my hair all over the place, and my coverlet draped around my shoulders for warmth, and my gigantic shadow against the wall drinking and hiccupping and sniggering whenever I did.

Finally I was so heavy-eyed and clumsy I could scarcely find my mouth, and deciding that my body had stomached all that it was capable of, I rolled the glass awkwardly to the floor and slid down beneath the blankets before sleep overpowered me.

I did not dream that night, indeed it is doubtful whether I stirred, for the first thing I knew was Jamie shaking my shoulder.

'Wakey, Mama — Jamie hungy.'

I forced my eyes open to see his anxious little face peering down at me.

We were late for breakfast but fortunately David had laid the table, and with Miriam's help had prepared the hot gruel and the oatcakes, so everyone was eating when Jamie and I eventually entered the kitchen. David explained that we had been very late the night before, but Miriam flashed me a venomous look. If Mr Starr could arise on time after a late night, why could not Beth Wood also?

I must have looked a wreck, for my head felt as heavy as lead, my mouth tasted foul, and my eye-lids would insist upon drooping over my eyes. But I cared not for discomfort. A way had been found to escape from Lucifer and his fiendish mind so I feared him no longer.

Unfortunately, although sleep came easily at night, lethargy began to dominate my waking hours, and I no longer had the energy or the patience with which I was normally blessed. Cooking was a burden, housework became a dreary chore, and I found myself snapping at Jamie, and falling asleep beside the fire of an evening, long before it was time for bed.

David was silent, puzzled and watchful, and on the fifth night all the bottles had disappeared from the larder shelf.

'Where are they? What have you done with them?' I stormed at him from the open doorway of his room.

He was sitting at his desk, which was under the window, and was still clad in his day clothes although it was past eleven o'clock. A book lay open in front of him and he raised his eyes from the pages and gazed back at me calmly.

'Beth, that is not the way,' he said. 'It is the way of weakness not of strength, and it will ruin you.'

'Rather ruination that way than by Lucifer's insidious poison. Where are the bottles? I will have them!'

'You cannot for they are empty,' he replied, 'I have poured the entire contents away.'

'No!' I sank down on his bed, my world falling about me, for without the sweet alcoholic stupor of the past nights I was lost. 'How could you do such a thing!' I whispered fiercely. 'Nothing can save me now — nothing!'

'If you do not care for my first suggestion there is still another path we can take. Let the church help you, Beth. No,' he went on quickly, as I jerked my head in violent denial, 'hear me out. We can but try this and see if it helps. Tomorrow I shall see the parson and ask for his blessing, and you and the boy must accompany me to church. Then I want you to wear this.' He held out a small gold cross and chain. 'It belonged to my mother. Put it on now and wear it always.'

'Lucas Silver gives Jamie a leather necklet with a black bean on it, and you give me a chain and cross. Does one superstitious bauble cancel out the other?'

'You will wear it,' he repeated, and limped across to where I sat and hung the chain around my neck.

It felt cold against my skin but I felt no emotion, no stirring of strength or comfort, only desolation.

'Is that it? Your piece of magic to oust his? I think you have taken on more than you know.' I rose and walked stiffly to the door. 'If you should hear screams again do not let them disturb you. You will have to accept my nightmares, as I must, from now on.'

'And this.' He ignored my remark and went back for his book. 'Take this Bible and read a chapter from the New Testament every night, start now with Matthew, then sleep with the Book beneath your pillow and ask God to help you.'

As I did not move he had to cross the room to reach me.

'Take it, Beth, and try to pray, for one can fight evil with good if only you would accept the fact.'

'I can accept nothing except that Silver's power is more than human, and I do not know if there is a God at all,' I said stonily, my solace gone and a book and a piece of jewellery given me as compensation.

'Then I shall pray for you.'

David closed the door softly behind me and I went to my room determined to stall for time and stay awake all night, if that were possible. But after reading the first chapter of the Gospel According to St Matthew, I was so bored with all the begatting and queer-sounding names, that my eyes closed despite my efforts to keep them open, and I knew no more.

Strangely, I was not disturbed that night and the Bible lay beneath my pillow from then on.

8

We went to church, Jamie and I, to have the devil purged from our souls. David accompanied us across the fields to the little grey building on the outskirts of the village.

I had not been so far away from the house before and found myself glancing suspiciously from left to right, expecting prying eyes and clacking tongues, or even to see the black figure of Lucas Silver arising from behind a bush, barring our way with malignant wrath. But we saw no one at that hour, the labourers all being indoors for their evening meal.

On the way David pointed out to me the Gritt's dwelling, and 'twas a ramshackle affair with mouldering thatch and sacking nailed across one of the two windows for lack of glass.

'One day they shall be adequately

housed,' he told me. 'If I can but make a small profit off the land, my first consideration will be for that family. They have served me faithfully, and my brother before me.' He sighed. 'They fare better these last years since they have fewer mouths to feed, but the family graves are a pathetic sight in the church-yard.'

He showed me the graves as we neared the church, and it was a sad sight, indeed, with two other sons and three daughters taken from Samuel and Miriam in the fateful year of 'seventy-one, all within the space of a fortnight. Poor things, no wonder they were so miserable, they had reason enough for gloom.

'Our family plot is over there.' David indicated with his head. 'All the Starrs gone save one, and that one shining but dimly, I fear.'

'Have faith, David,' I replied, 'you must practise what you preach.'

He shrugged and led the way down the path to where a little, white-haired parson awaited us in the porch.

David was so solemn about the whole business that I wished that I, too, could share his faith. He and Parson prayed together, quietly, earnestly, but I, after one look at the frail, elderly man, knew that he would be totally incompetent against Lucas Silver. I needed somebody with strength, with a power to match Lucifer's own and to vanquish him. David and his companion were undoubtedly good, but they lacked too many other qualities.

I sat with bowed head, trying to think positively, but once again Silver won and I seemed to hear his mocking laughter blotting out the murmured prayers beside me.

Discomforted, I glanced down at Jamie, who sat between David and myself, his short legs stuck out before him, and was surprised by the expression on the child's face.

He was not at ease either, one fist clutching at his chest where his 'beany' hung, his eyes rolling, wide and troubled. I knew that he was trying not to cry so I put an arm round him, cuddling him to me.

'It's all right, darling, we are going home soon,' I whispered, wondering what thoughts were passing through his childish brain.

Jamie had never been inside a church before, except as a tiny babe for his baptism, and no doubt the high raftered ceiling and stark walls intimidated him, as well as the hush, and the austerity of the empty pews. It was not a cosy church, nor a pretty one, with a single stained glass window above the altar, and narrow, plain glass apertures down the sides which filtered a cold grey light into the building.

'It won't be long now,' and I hugged him, but the old parson looked round, and David frowned at me for speaking.

Parson blessed us both, patting our heads with a shaky hand as if we were prize cattle. Maybe it would help, I thought doubtfully, but Jamie shrunk from the man's touch as if the clergyman would hurt him.

I do not know what explanation David gave for our presence there, nor did I wait for questions afterwards. Smiling a brief farewell, I fairly ran from the place, with Jamie scampering at my heels like a hare from the hounds.

'Come on up, Jamie boy,' I cried, lifting the child on to my shoulders and galloping with him across the fields.

It was good to be out in the clean, fresh air, away from the fusty atmosphere of the church and the dark oak pews; away from the trembling voice of the old man and the hard stuffed hassocks. Outside the fields were abrim with life and growing things and I felt suddenly uplifted.

'Gee up, Mama — quick, quick!' yelled Jamie, and I ran until breathless, ending up laughing and exhausted in the side yard.

Miss Hannah was in the kitchen awaiting our arrival.

'I wondered where you were,' she said, smiling at our flushed faces, as I swung the little boy to the ground. 'There is a letter for you, Mrs Wood, from my sister. She sent me one, also, and it was such a pleasant evening I decided to walk up with it so that you would have it today.'

I thanked her and took the letter, but there was no time to read for supper had to be prepared and then David came in, and Miss Hannah was invited to join us. So it was not until later that night that I first had the chance to survey the contents.

Miss Bloster was brief.

'Mr Silver visited two days before Christmas,' she wrote, 'and I fear, Elizabeth, that he was greatly vexed to find you gone. He is an odd man and I can understand your fear of him, but nonetheless, I found it in my heart to be sorry for him. He wants his son so badly, my dear.

'However, I have held my tongue up until now and shall continue to do so, although I beg you to reconsider your decision. It is natural for a man to want to see his child, and to watch it grow and progress. Could you not come to some arrangement with him? There is also a letter from Meredith which arrived yesterday, and I hasten to send it on to you with my best wishes and sincere hope that you and the boy are happy and in good health.'

Angrily I crumpled the pages in my fist. Now he was working on Miss Bloster. Reconsider my decision? After all that I had been through? How dare she preach at me!

'Bad news?' David queried from across the hearth.

'Hardly good!' I snapped, turning to the letter from Merry which Miss Bloster had enclosed.

'Darling Elizabeth, I do entreat you to listen to me. Lucas is very, very angry with you and making me suffer, too. Oh, dearest, do take Barnaby back home, or better still, bring him to London and let us be a family once more.

'I miss you, Elizabeth, and find it

terribly strange not knowing where you are, or where I can reach you. And Lucas wants his son, dearest. I do not care whether I see him again, or not, but Lucas wants the boy and will not rest until he knows your whereabouts. He wants to train Barnaby for the Act, Elizabeth, and the younger he starts the better it will be.

'Do not defy him any longer, I beg. His wrath is awful to behold and it is causing great harm to our performances. He does not concentrate so well now, Elizabeth, he thinks always of you, and when he reads my mind I get terrible head-aches — it is almost as if his anger is burning into my brain.

'Lucas has had a bad time of late, with no particular enthusiasm shown him on the continent, and now the Prince of Wales is losing interest, and the London audiences are so fickle they are off seeking entertainment elsewhere. We know that having a child in the Act will add to the novelty of our performance, so we *must* have our son, Elizabeth.

'Lucas is irritable with Cousin Grace, and shuts himself away at night and the atmosphere is not pleasant. Do think of the harm you are doing us all and come back to us. Come to London — for Cousin Grace is very frail; she picked up the infection I had and has not been well for months. I do not believe she can live for long. Oh, come, Elizabeth! Say that Barnaby is your foster child and you can both stay here with us and we will all be happy again. I am your sister, dearest, and I need you. Do not disappoint me, your loving Merry.'

I tore the pages of her letter across and threw them onto the flames before slumping in my chair, head in hands.

'Tell me what has upset you.' David's voice roused me and I lifted my head to stare back at him.

'One man,' I answered stonily.

'This Silver fellow?'

'Who else?'

'What do they say about him?'

'That he wants Jamie — that he will not rest until he finds him. Silver wants to use him on stage. Can you imagine, David? That devil will exhaust his brain and tax his little body to the limit. I tell you, he shall not have Jamie for his evil purposes, he shall not!'

'But you are safe here, Beth, and you have not had any more nightmares. Maybe you are free of him?'

'Never! Now Merry suffers. For how long can I bear her pleading words and miserable accusations? You see, Lucifer is venting his wrath on her. If he cannot reach me he intends hurting my sister. Can I live with that knowledge, David?'

'Dear Lord, what a mess!' He ran his fingers through his hair. 'Is he hurting her physically? Can she not run away? Would your friend Miss Bloster not offer her sanctuary?'

'Silver will not let Merry go,' I

answered grimly, 'she is his last tie with me.'

But there was yet another link with the man which I was to discover that very night.

I slept but fitfully, tossing and turning, remembering Merry's pathetic words and wondering what could be done about her. And as I lay there, half-asleep, Jamie began stirring in his cot, and I heard him chuckle and mutter in his dreams.

I smiled and lifted myself upon one elbow, wondering what pleasant visions he was seeing. Then he began to speak more clearly and my body froze as I realised exactly what was going on.

Lucas Silver was getting through to Jamie.

I fumbled for the candle beside my bed and lit it, my hands a-tremble, then flinging on my night robe I fled across the bare boards to stare down at the sleeping child. He was asleep, I was certain, although his eyes were open, staring wide and luminous at the ceiling. Jamie was smiling, clutching at his 'beany' with one hand, waving the other small fist before him.

'Nice,' he was saying, 'nice, Jamie like it here.' Then there was some gibberish followed by, 'Pussies 'n' cows 'n' Uncle Daydee.'

Lucifer was speaking to him, asking questions about where we lived. The child could not yet say Starrling, and would not know our address, but Silver would guess it was a farm and if he caught the name David Starr, or Hannah Bloster, it would not be long before he traced us.

Gently I began to sing a lullaby which Mother had sung to me in the old days, at the same time stroking Jamie's body, and recapturing his waving arm and tucking it down beneath the covers.

'Away in a manger, no crib for a
    bed
The little Lord Jesus laid down
    His sweet head

The stars in the bright sky
Looked down where He lay
The little Lord Jesus asleep on the
    hay.'

'Go to sleep, my darling,' I crooned, 'sleep sweet till morning. There, there, my baby, rest and sleep.'

Jamie muttered once more and closed his eyes, then turned over on his side and snuggled against his pillow.

'There, my darling, go to sleep.' I stroked his shoulder until his breathing deepened and I was certain that he was sound asleep.

Then I turned and went back towards my bed but as I did so Lucifer's voice rang in my head, so fiercely that I could have sworn he spoke aloud in the room.

'WHERE ARE YOU? ELIZABETH, TELL ME WHERE YOU ARE. WHAT PLACE IS THAT? THE NAME — TELL ME THE NAME.'

I shut my eyes tightly, feeling my head throbbing as if it would burst.

'WHERE ARE YOU?'

Don't think! Don't tell him! Think of something — quick! Think of something to blot out his signal.

'WHERE ARE YOU, ELIZABETH? I WILL KNOW.'

It was no good, his voice was coming through urgent and strong. How to blank it out? How smother it?

Grabbing the Bible from beneath my pillow, and holding it so tightly against my chest that my heart thumped against its cover, I began babbling the Lord's Prayer, which we said every morning before breakfast. I jabbered on and on, repeating the familiar phrases until Silver's voice faded.

I, too, became silent and there was not a sound in the room save for Jamie's steady breathing.

The relief was intense. So jubilant did I feel that I could not sleep and had to rush across the landing to inform David of my success. I had won! Lucifer was vanquished and need never be feared again.

I opened David's door quietly, not wanting to awaken him too abruptly, and then gasped at what I saw.

He was sitting at his desk, a tiny stump of candle still flickering beside him, his hands clasped, his head bowed. He was praying.

'David!' My whisper startled him and he spun round, his face white and drawn.

'What is it, Beth?' He stood up and limped towards me. 'Have you dreamed again? Was it another nightmare?'

'No.' I stared up into his weary face. 'Do you do this every night? Keep this vigil for me?'

He smiled. 'It is not difficult for I do not sleep well. Tell me, Beth, why have you come?'

'To tell you that Silver tried to contact Jamie, he was asking him questions about where we lived, and then he tried me again and I was able to withstand him.' I stopped, biting at my lip. 'But it wasn't me at all, was it? I felt so proud of the fact that I had won

— wanted to tell you about it — but it was your doing. You have prayed for me nightly haven't you?'

He nodded, taking my hands in his. 'You are cold, go back to bed.' And he began to lead me to the other room. 'I can do nothing for you save pray, and if that helps I shall continue to do it. I cannot bear to see your distress, my dear.'

Not knowing how to answer that, I went with him silently back to my room.

'Good night, Beth, and sleep well. I told you that prayers were sometimes answered. Oh, ye of little faith,' he mocked gently, and went out shutting the door behind him.

★   ★   ★

David's prayers seemed to help me but I was still frightened for Jamie.

'What about removing that cursed bean?' asked David, two evenings' later, looking wan from his sleepless nights, whilst I felt hollow-eyed and miserable from lack of rest. I did little more than doze now, immediately awake whenever Jamie moved or grunted, ready to attack the moment Silver tried communicating with the boy again.

'Presumably that necklace is his connection with the child?' David said. 'If I removed it he would not be able to reach Jamie.'

'Do not try.' I shook my head vigorously. 'I told you what happened at home when I tried to take it off.'

'But Silver had hypnotised you then, Beth, into believing that you would be hurt if you touched it. I have had no such experience with the man and am certain no harm will befall me.'

'No.' David had been hurt enough in life with his crippled leg and unhappy past, he should not suffer more. He was so kind, too, bearing my burden as if it were his own, why should he suffer more for me? 'Leave it, David. The wretched thing is almost part of Jamie now, he would be greatly upset if you removed his 'beany'.'

'I should like to try,' he answered stubbornly. 'If it will save you from further anguish the effort will be worthwhile. Let us go up now whilst the boy sleeps.'

David took the large scissors from the drawer in the kitchen dresser, and we went quietly upstairs into the darkened room. As David bent to cut the leather I held the lamp high above his head. But as he leaned over Jamie, the child awoke and screamed, frightened, no doubt, by the two of us standing over him and the flash of steel in the man's hand.

There was savage hate in his normally clear blue eyes and even as David stood back, putting the scissors behind him, Jamie caught hold of his free hand and bit it, sinking his small sharp teeth into David's flesh. We both cried out, the man in pain, and I in anger. Then I lunged forward, unthinking, and slapped Jamie hard across his face.

'No, Beth! He did not mean it — can't you see that he is not himself?' David pulled me away as the boy burst into tears.

It was some time before we were calm and I was able to take the shrinking child into my arms, comforting him, whilst David bound up his wound with his handkerchief.

'He will have forgotten by morning,' said David. 'Stay with him till he sleeps, Beth.'

I held the small, shivering body close, murmuring endearments, until his sobs died and he snuggled against me, asleep once more.

'My own stupid fault,' David remarked. 'I should have listened to you.'

'He was possessed.' I stared up at the man, finding it difficult to accept that my loving Jamie had, for one brief moment, turned into a wild beast.

'Forget it, Beth. Do not speak a word of this tomorrow. It was a nightmare and we will never refer to it again.'

I nodded, laying the sleeping child back into his bed and pulling the covers over him.

'I shall not speak of it, but I shall never forget.'

The next morning David's hand was painfully swollen and he kept it bandaged for a week. He told the Gritts that he had burned his hand whilst making up the fire, and fortunately, Jamie had no recollection of that disturbing event.

So the new year progressed, with Lucas Silver still occasionally trying to make contact but succeeding not at all now that I knew how to banish him. My own strength was all the greater, filled with a hatred so intense that fear for myself had vanished. But I worried increasingly about Jamie, and the appalling certainty that Lucifer was gradually gaining a hold over his little son.

9

During that summer I discovered something about myself; I discovered my own power, the force within me which Lucas Silver must have noticed when we first met, and about which I knew nothing.

The knowledge came to me in the simplest way one sunny morning as I was tending the garden. Such a splendid garden it was, too, by then. My second year of hard work was providing bounty in plenty, and I kept the household and Miss Hannah supplied with fresh vegetables, and fruit in season throughout the summer months and on into the winter.

That morning I was collecting up the first strawberries, and so sweet and juicy were they, that I longed for Jamie to join me in my feast.

He was sturdier, more independent

now in his third year, and I allowed him greater freedom, so that he roamed the fields, sometimes not coming near me until meal times. Jamie was a sensible child, old beyond his years, and after so long at Starrling, I knew that he was safe in a physical sense and allowed him to wander at will, so long as he stayed within sight and sound of the house.

That morning I ate the strawberries, not knowing where the boy was, about to call for him, when he appeared through the hedge and scampered across to where I was bending over the straw-covered beds.

'Yes, Mama, Jamie here — what you want?' Then his eyes lit up and he was on hands and knees searching for his own delicacies.

I smiled, then straightened with a jolt. 'What did you say, Jamie? You heard me calling?'

He grunted, his mouth full. 'Jamie, Jamie, you called. And Jamie come quick and find lovely berries.' He grabbed me round the knees, pressing his grubby face against my breeches. 'Thank you, Mama — Jamie glad!'

I patted his head thoughtfully, and then he pulled away and continued his searching. Could it be true? Had I this same strange power of communication and not known it until now? Why had I not discovered it before?

Was it, perhaps, that Jamie had inherited Silver's sensitivity, and now that he was older and we were so close I could make contact with him? Merry and Father had been the two dearest people during my young adult life, but I had had no such communication with them.

Merry could not possess it, or she and Silver would not have needed to write letters when he was in America. He could take over her mind when she was bodily in his presence, but, unlike me, he would have no contact with her when they were apart.

But Jamie definitely had 'it', and so had I. During the next few days I tried further communication with him, feeling my wings, so to speak, and the child responded every time, eventually becoming quite irritated.

'Must not always call Jamie!' he told me, stamping his foot. 'Jamie busy and Mama calling, calling. Jamie not like.'

'Sorry, darling, I don't mean to disturb you but just want to know where you are.' I knelt down and hugged him. 'But I won't do it again — at least not often. Promise.'

'Good, Jamie not like,' he said again.

I tried it on David, unfairly calling him from the fields. But fortunately he did not answer, for I do not know what excuse I could have offered had he come hurrying back to the house in the middle of a busy morning's work. Then I remembered how Lucas Silver had looked deep into his victim's eyes, bending them to his will, and I wondered if I possessed this same visual command.

Job! This was a splendid chance to right that old matter of the bean. Although he was more relaxed at meal times, he still refused to sit beside Jamie, or to go near him. Yes, Job. Perhaps I could make him forget his fear of the bean and become friendly with the little boy again. But I would have to confront him on his own, and could not hope to carry out my plan with his suspicious mother peering over my shoulder.

Tuesday was a very hot day, building up for the thunder which would not break for another twelve hours. Jamie and I carried a flagon of cider, which I had kept chilled in the larder, and a basket of hot meat pies and baked potatoes, out to the workers in the field. David was working flat out in the hay field, desperate to get the grass dried and into the barn before the storm broke. There was no time to come up to the house for lunch, so we carried food and drink out to the field, and the workers snatched a twenty-minute break before continuing with their labours.

As I had hoped, they were all strung

out across the meadow and Job was at the far end, lifting and turning the hay with a fork before loading it onto the wagon.

'Job!' I called, leaving Jamie beside David and moving across to speak to the big fellow alone. 'Job, I have brought food and a nice cold drink for you.'

He looked up, pausing momentarily as I approached, and as he stared at me I held his gaze, whereas before I had always turned away, finding his squat, pocked features and heavy jowl an unpleasing sight. Now I smiled into his eyes.

'You must make friends with Jamie again, Job, for he likes you and you really like him, don't you?'

He nodded, his black, pig-like eyes intent on mine.

'And you must not fear that necklace any more, Job, it is but a silly bean and you need not be afraid of it.'

He nodded again, his mouth hanging open and saliva beginning to trickle from one corner.

'You are a good lad, a sensible and kind fellow, and that bean will not worry you any more, understand?'

He grinned and licked his mouth and nodded more vigorously.

'Good Job, now come and eat, you must be famished.'

We strolled back to the others, who were resting beneath the trees on the edge of the field. And, filled with elation, I stared straight at Miriam.

'I shall be coming down to help you this afternoon as soon as Jamie wakes from his nap,' I told her.

She jerked her head at me and I met her small, spiteful eyes squarely. Again, something I had avoided up until now, for we both disliked each other and had avoided visual contact at all times.

'Master David can do with all the help he can get, so I intend being here and we will get along famously together.'

I smiled at her, forcing my lips back

from my teeth, willing her to respond positively.

'Reckon we could do with you, Mrs,' she answered, 'and more of your cider, at that! It tastes real good when you're parched.'

Miriam smiled back at me with difficulty for she was not used to the action. But it was a smile nonetheless, and I saw old Samuel stare in wonder at his wife's shiny face.

'Right.' I shot David a triumphant look before reaching for Jamie's hand. 'Come, my boy, we'll go back for our food and rest, then we'll join these good people and show them what our muscles are like.'

He chortled and gave a little skip, for he had long wanted to accompany David on the wagon but I had kept him apart from the Gritts as an act of diplomacy. We left Job grinning and Miriam nodding agreeably, whilst the two older men sat in silent astonishment as we departed.

'What the devil have you done?'

asked David that evening, as, close to midnight, we prepared to leave the kitchen and make our weary way to bed. 'Have you bewitched mother and son? I have never seen Miriam so cheerful, and Job was giving Jamie a piggy-back on the way home tonight.'

'You can call it that.' I spun round and stared into his face. 'Look at me, David, now it's your turn! Look deep into my eyes and do exactly what I say!'

I was laughing as his hand shot out and grasped my wrist so tightly that his fingers bit into my flesh.

'Don't, David — you're hurting me!'

'Never look at me like that again.' He spoke through tight lips, his brows drawn together in anger.

'It was only a joke, I was teasing you,' I whimpered, rubbing at my wrist.

'Beth, something has changed you. What is it?' He took the lamp and held it near my face, his gaze wandering over my eyes, my hair, my mouth. 'Is it that man Silver? Has he got into you?'

'I don't know what you are talking

about, and move that lamp away, it's hot!' I stepped away from him, close to tears, his anger having jolted me to my senses. 'Can't you take a joke, David? Or are you so pious that you consider merriment a sin?'

'A joke!' He banged the lamp down so hard upon the table that the flame flickered, then he turned and took hold of my shoulders.

'Look at me, Beth.' Slowly I raised my eyes to his, feeling like a naughty child. 'That is better.' David's hands dropped from my shoulders and he sighed. 'For a moment you were a stranger and I saw the most terrible expression in your eyes. What got into you, girl? What were you playing at?'

'I was — ' I began, and then stopped as realisation hit me.

I was playing at being Lucas Silver, apeing the master, copying the man whom I detested. Shuddering, I bent forward across the table, clutching at its worn sides.

'I am a fool,' I whispered, 'thank

heavens you made me see it in time. I have his power, you see. I have recently discovered it and have been trying out my strength on different people.' I lifted my head and stared across to where David stood, white and silent, shocked by my confession. 'I can communicate with Jamie by thought, not words, and I made Job forget his fear of the bean, and I started on Miriam, too. But they were all good things, David, I meant no harm.'

'Not this time,' he answered slowly, 'but don't you see the danger? You practice this — this power of yours and you will become better and better at it, until like Silver you will be able to take possession of anybody's mind. But where will it end, Beth? When will the good finish and the evil begin? Where do you draw the line?'

'What do you mean? I would only ever use it for good purposes.'

'Would you? Would you really? And what if you were angry one day, driven to fury by someone? Would it not be easy in a flash of temper to hate them, or curse them, perhaps do them irreparable harm? Can you be so certain of your self-control, Beth?'

'No.' I shook my head. 'But I can, and will, use it against Lucas Silver if I am ever given the chance. I shall use it to protect Jamie, and you cannot stop me.'

My companion shrugged. 'Use it to help the child, if you must, but never test your skills on me, Beth. Dear heavens, how I wish we could rid ourselves of that devil forever and be left alone to live our lives in peace.'

'He won't give up until he has Jamie,' I said softly, 'and I am going to fight him every inch of the way. I'll not allow him to take my son away, David, I'll not!'

10

In August Merry came to Starrling. She wrote me a pitiful letter and I, guiltily aware of having ignored her first pleas, could not refuse her sanctuary.

'I am staying with Mr Arthur and his mother,' she wrote, in a spidery, erratic hand which was quite unlike her normal rounded script. 'I have run away from Lucas — he is a wicked, hateful man and I shall find no peace until I am safe with you, Elizabeth. Oh, come to me quickly, dearest, and rescue me. The Drews shelter me but I do not feel truly welcome, and Mrs Drew makes it clear that I am a burden on the household. I have asked Miss Bloster to forward this letter to you, and beg for your compassion. Please come soon, dearest, for Lucas may yet seek me out and he terrifies me. Your lost sister, Merry.'

It was a dramatic and pathetic letter which I could not disregard. What had happened to make her see Lucifer in his true light, I wondered grimly.

Unfortunately, it was the worst possible time of year for me to leave the farm; David and the Gritts could not labour without food, and the horse and wagon were needed daily in the fields. Tentatively I asked David if I could take the cart to fetch my sister, but he shook his head.

'Until the harvest is in I cannot allow you transport, Beth, and anyway, I would not want you to travel across the countryside on your own.'

'If the weather changes, may I go? You do not mind if she joins us? It is perhaps a great deal to ask, but I want to help her if I can.'

'Of course your sister may come, if she can stand the poverty.' He smiled crookedly. 'After the luxuries of that London house will she be able to adapt to the privations of Starrling?'

'Merry needs peace and a loving

home more than comforts,' I replied. 'I shall make a room ready for her. May she have the big one with the four-poster in it? I believe that is the only other bed in the place. And I shall write to her and warn her to expect me some time during the next few weeks.'

David nodded. 'Meredith may have that room. It was my parents' and later, Randolph's, so it will be pleasant to see it occupied again.'

'I shall put flowers there and polish up the floorboards and shine the windows. Once it is prettied up she will be delighted with it.'

There were even curtains up there, faded and dusty, to be sure, but of good material. Once I had cleaned and mended them they would look almost as good as new.

'I still do not want you travelling alone.' David returned to the subject which I had hoped was forgotten. 'You had better take Job with you when we are less busy.'

'I should not dream of spending the

journey in his company! Although he is kind to Jamie and means well, poor fellow, I cannot bear the sight of him. Do not worry, David, I am stronger and tougher than ever since wielding that pitchfork. Would you feel happier if I stuck a knife in my bodice?' I teased. 'Not that anyone would dare to molest me, with my gypsy looks and evil eye!'

He shook his head in exasperation, but he smiled at the same time and I knew then that he would let me go.

'If the weather breaks,' he said, 'or when we have the harvest safely in, then you may go to fetch Meredith. Inform her also that you will spend the night there, for I will not allow you to sleep in the cart as Samuel did. You leave here one day and return the next, and I shall not rest until you are safely back at Starrling once more,' he added quietly.

'No harm will befall me,' I answered, full of confidence, excited by the thought of such an adventure.

Confidence had come flooding back once I knew that I could defend myself and Jamie against Lucas Silver; he had not bothered us for a long time, and I felt fit and happy from my out-of-door living. All that remained for perfect serenity was to have my sister with us at Starrling.

For more than a year I had not left the farm, not even to visit the market or the neighbouring villages, and the thought of visiting my home town was elating.

'Perhaps I could call on Miss Bloster? I should love to see her again, and all the changes she has made to my former home.' Then I stopped, hand to mouth. 'But I cannot.'

Of course I could not see my old friend, nor pass through the town in daylight. For not only had I still to guard my own and Jamie's safety, but soon Merry must be sheltered from Lucifer's far-reaching clutches.

I would have to time my journey so that I arrived at the Drew's house after dark, and see that we left at dawn next morning, in order to be through the town and away before sunrise. Merry would have to be warned that all packing must be done before my arrival, and knowing her, doubtless she would have luggage in plenty. Or had her escape been totally unprepared? She would have to wake early without dawdling and be ready to leave with me at an uncomfortably early hour.

Some of my excitement dimmed at the prospect before me, and I hoped that my sister had altered her ways, and would be more co-operative than she had been the last time I saw her. But, judging from her letters, she had changed and no doubt her unfortunate circumstances had made her a less selfish and exasperating person.

Poor Merry. My conscience smote me, for here I was already thinking uncivil thoughts and criticising her in my mind.

'I shall make her room really welcoming,' I told David, 'and I look forward to seeing her again. She altered so much during her years with Lucas

Silver that I hope she will learn to be my little sister again, whom I once most dearly loved.'

'Do not expect too much at the beginning,' he said soberly. 'Meredith has experienced much sorrow of late, and you must be prepared for a different person to the one you last saw. She sounds unhappy and ill. Do you know what ails her?'

'She picked up an infection in Italy, which I believed to be cured. It was some time ago, shortly after Jamie was born, so I presume she is sick at heart, more than anything else. All that magic-ing about with Lucas Silver has no doubt taxed her health. What Merry needs is plenty of good farm produce, and buckets of fresh air, and here she will receive both in abundance.' I smiled across at my companion. 'Thank you, David, I am grateful to you for taking on another member of my family without complaint.'

'If Meredith is anything like her sister she will make a most welcome addition to our little community,' he remarked gallantly, and I was warmed, as always, by his infrequent compliments.

We arranged that he would leave his door open in case Jamie cried out in the night, and I tucked my Bible beneath the child's pillow when making up the beds that last morning. Miss Hannah was to have my bed, so that Jamie would not sleep alone, and as we had not been disturbed by Silver for a long while, I felt reasonably sure that all would remain calm during my absence.

Miss Hannah moved up to the house on the morning I left, to care for the family whilst I was away, and to take charge of Jamie. It was particularly hard leaving him, for we had never been separated before, not even for a day, and he could not understand why I must go away from him.

'Jamie too,' he said, holding up his arms as I stood wrapping my shawl about me, ready for the journey.

'Darling, not this time.' I knelt to hug him, and felt his small body quivering as he strained against me.

'Mama not go! Not leave Jamie!' he cried, burrowing his head into my shoulder.

Miss Hannah clucked and fussed like a worried hen, and I was almost in tears as I tried to explain.

'Mama is going to fetch your Aunt Merry, sweetheart, and oh, what fun we will have when she comes! For she is pretty and gay and always laughing, Jamie. And we'll take her for walks and you can show her all the animals, and help to look after her. Let me go now, darling, and I shall quickly be home again.'

'Not go — not go!' He clung to me like a little limpet.

David came across the yard then, leading the horse and cart, calling to me to make ready.

'You go to Uncle David,' I said thankfully, 'and keep him company whilst Mama is away. You will be two men together taking care of the place. Now isn't that a fine idea? And men don't cry, Jamie.'

David came forward and swung the boy up onto his shoulders. 'You will have a good view from here,' he said, 'and can wave Mama goodbye. Tomorrow we'll be here waiting to wave again when she comes up the drive.'

Hastily I bundled myself up into the cart, and taking the reins in my hands I clicked my tongue to Caesar and we began to trundle away from the little group in the yard.

I took a last look over my shoulder at Miss Hannah's square, solid body next to David's slim one, and the bright curls above my son's red face, then I turned my eyes steadfastly away and started on my journey west.

I was late arriving. Although I had enough food and drink for both directions, the horse had to be rested at intervals and I lost my way twice. The road ran mainly due west, but some sign posts were badly weathered and difficult to read, and I wandered for almost an hour down one country lane, and found myself on a rough farm track another time. But once through East Grinstead I was sure of my bearings and arrived at the Drews just as night was falling.

The Drews, in the politest way, were delighted to be rid of Merry.

Mr Arthur opened the door to me, whispering that my sister was in bed, for she had tired of waiting for me.

'Miss Meredith is not well, I fear, and has suffered dreadfully at the hands of that brutish man.'

Whilst he went out to tend Caesar, I saw his mother briefly in her sitting-room and thanked her for looking after Merry.

'Such goings-on,' remarked the lady, jerking her head in disdain. 'London is a city of vice, Elizabeth, and what your poor father would have thought of all this business, I dare not imagine.'

Feeling annoyed at the fact that Merry had blurted out more than was necessary, and dreading the thought of all the gossip which would surely circulate after our departure, I informed Mrs Drew that I would be taking my sister away very early the following morning.

'I have a charming home now,' I said briskly, 'where Merry will have the chance to settle down to a normal, carefree life at last. But we must start early as I live in the county of Hampshire and 'tis a long journey from here.'

That would put Lucas Silver off the scent, should he ever come seeking information.

'She is not well,' said Mr Arthur mournfully, reappearing as I made to leave his mother.

His hair was beginning to grow thin on top and I wondered how I could ever have contemplated marriage with such a gloomy person.

'Show me to her room, if you would be so kind.' I smiled determinedly into his face. 'We will let ourselves out tomorrow without disturbing you, for we must make an early start,' I said.

Merry did not look well. She greeted me with pathetic eagerness, rising from her bed and flinging her arms about my neck as if she would never let me go. But her shoulders felt brittle beneath my hands, and her hair was lank and greasy against my cheek.

'Why, Merry love, how thin you are!' I held her away from me, and her great violet eyes stared back at me in the candle-light, with shadows beneath them like purple bruises. 'Have you not been eating properly?'

'I have not been eating or sleeping.' Her mouth twitched and she clasped my hands to her chest. 'But I don't care now that you've found me. Take me away, Elizabeth, oh, take me away with you and do not ever leave me again.'

'I won't, dearest, and I shall have you as fat as a little partridge in a month's time.'

Merry slept well but I did not, wondering all night long just how much she had suffered at the hands of Lucas Silver. Only one thought comforted me;

my sister, safe at Starrling, would never share the fate of that poor first Mrs Silver.

We got away soon after five next morning, the old horse seeming to know that he was on his way home and pulling the wagon with markedly more enthusiasm than he had shown the day before. Merry, too, was no trouble, and awoke and followed me without complaint. We did not stop to eat until we were far out of town, but then I pulled up at the side of the road and we finished the last of the oatcakes which I had brought with me from the farm.

There was still heavy cloud about, and the soft south-westerly wind promised more rain, so I allowed Ceasar to make his own pace, knowing that David would not be in any hurry for the cart.

'What made you decide to leave Mr Silver?' I asked, once we had eaten and were continuing with our journey. 'Do you wish to talk about it, or would you rather forget the wretched past?'

'I do not mind.'

Merry was looking fresher that morning, obviously uplifted at the thought of beginning a new life. I had tied her hair back with a piece of ribbon which helped to hide its appalling condition, and the fresh air had blown some colour into her face.

'It is like a bad dream, Elizabeth, from which I have now awoken, and finding you here beside me has caused all my troubles to fade away.' She put out her hand and patted my arm. 'Lucas was cruel, he no longer cared for me, nor wanted me, yet he would not let me go, either.' She spoke in a clear, sing-song manner, without expression. 'Cousin Grace discovered us in bed one night when she came to my room unexpectedly, and she was so angry she all but threw us out into the street there and then.' Merry gave a high little giggle. 'She did look funny, Elizabeth, with her face all red and blotchy and that silly lace cap bobbing about on top! So Lucas and I had to leave next morning, and I left all my clothes and lovely jewels behind, and we went to live on his houseboat.'

'Houseboat?'

'He lived there before and kept it all the time he was with Cousin Grace. Luckily for us he did, I do not know where we would have gone else. It is on the river at Chelsea, a horrible place.' For the first time revulsion showed in her voice. 'I hated it there! Smelly and dark and filled with dusty books and all his dirty animals. Oh, I did not like it at all! And the filthy river water went slap, slap all day and night against the sides of the boat, and there was noise from the road, and chatter and cries and shouts from the people living alongside. There is quite a community of water folk, Elizabeth, and they are a loud-mouthed, ignorant lot. I do not think Lucas liked it, either, but he was away a good deal and made me stay behind.' She shivered.

'Was there a child on the boat? A little girl called Susie?' I asked. Her mother and sister were dead but what had happened to the other girl, Lucas Silver's eldest daughter?

'Susie?' Merry stared at me. 'I've never heard of her. It was only me and I was so lonely and miserable, I could not stand it, Elizabeth.' She clutched at my arm, pressing her face against my sleeve.

'Why was Mr Silver cruel to you, Merry? Did he beat you?' I hated even to think about the man, but it was good for Merry to talk, to unload her mind of such memories, and hopefully be free of Lucifer forever.

'He would not let me go,' she repeated, 'although I became ill there because the damp air did not suit me. Lucas never touched me but then he did not need to, one look from him was quite enough.' Suddenly she began to weep. 'Do not go on at me so, Elizabeth! I do not wish to talk about him any more. Is it not enough that I ran away, that I am at last rid of him? Why do you keep asking questions and making me remember?'

'Merry sweet, I'm sorry.' I put my free arm round her trembling shoulders. 'Don't cry, dear, we won't talk about him any more. I did not mean to upset you, don't cry, I beg. Look — we are coming to Ashdown Forest — is it not pretty? I shall pick you some heather to put in your bodice.'

I pulled up Caesar and jumped down from the cart to pluck a great bunch of heathers for her, pink and deep mauve and white. Merry smiled as she clasped them to her bosom, tears forgotten.

Dear heavens, I thought, looking up at her streaked face and red-rimmed eyes, what will David and Jamie think of her? Wishing that I had not made so much of his 'gay and laughing' aunt, I tucked myself up beside her again, thankful that Jamie was too young to voice his thoughts, and David too much of a gentleman to do so.

'You are going to be so spoilt, Merry,' I went on brightly, 'and your room is ready waiting for you. Sparsely furnished, I'm afraid, but clean and cosy, and we'll have such fun together, just wait and see!'

She sniffed and swallowed, cradling the heather on her lap. 'This David you mentioned earlier, are you married to him?'

'Why, no, Merry,' I smiled, 'he is my employer, and a good, kind man, besides.'

She nodded. 'You spoke of him in such a familiar tone that I thought perhaps you were wed.'

Was she married to Mr Silver? I wondered, glancing down at her ringless hands. But I dared not ask, not yet. And where did he go so often when she was left alone? Did he still continue with his performances, perhaps with that Arabella whom he had taken with him to America? Surely with the contacts he had made over the years he would be able to continue with his Act without Cousin Grace's patronage? Many questions to be asked, many things still to know, but the answers would have to wait. First my sister must be given a stable and contented way of life, then, maybe, she would be able to talk without upsetting herself with memories.

'How is Barnaby?' she asked suddenly. 'Have you told him that I am coming?'

I hesitated, unsure of how to deal with her. My words would have to be chosen with care.

'He is very well, Merry, and I have told him that his aunt is coming.' I shot a quick look at her. 'He thinks that I am his mother, you see, and whilst he is so young it is better that he does not know the truth.'

Merry nodded, and I breathed more easily.

'I never wanted him,' she said, 'but Lucas longed for a son. You did make him cross, Elizabeth, when you disappeared like that and then he became angry with me.' Big tears began to roll down her cheeks again, and she threw the heather out of the cart and lifted her skirt to wipe her nose. 'Oh, dearie me, you will think me a fool and a cry-baby, but I do feel so depressed I cannot help myself.' And she snuffled and blew into the folds of her gown.

'Merry, use this.' I handed her my handkerchief, fighting repulsion for the distracted girl at my side.

Quickly, scarcely waiting to draw breath, I began to tell her about Starrling; about the house and the animals, my garden, and the new kittens in the barn. I talked for what seemed like hours, boring her, no doubt, by my unceasing chatter, but it stopped her from talking, possibly from thinking, and certainly from crying.

As my voice became hoarse and words dried up, I saw the chimneys of Miss Hannah's cottage in the distance, and the line of fir trees which bordered this side of Starrling.

'Almost there, Merry,' I announced huskily, 'in a few minutes we shall be home.'

Jamie was waiting by the rusty gates, his little face breaking into a great beam of delight as we rounded the bend and entered the rutted drive.

'Mama! Mama!' He shouted, and ran to the cart, where I lifted him up and held him closely, unwilling ever to let him go. He, at least, was greatly loved and would always know it. After a while he wriggled free from my embrace and settled himself between us, and I introduced him to Merry.

She smiled down at him and took his hand. 'My, what a fine strong lad you are,' she said.

Jamie beamed again and snuggled against me, and we drove up to the house where Miss Hannah was waiting, her round face wreathed in smiles.

'Welcome home, Mrs Wood,' she called, 'and you, too, Miss Meredith. We are that glad to see you safely back.'

Then David limped around the corner of the barn, and I knew that he had been hovering there all afternoon, finding work to keep him within earshot of the drive.

Happiness radiated from him as he patted Caesar's neck, but all he said was,

'Bring your sister in, Beth, she must be tired.'

That was a happy evening spent around the big table in the kitchen, set with the ham which I had cooked especially for Merry's arrival, and a great bowl of fresh salad from my garden, and a fruit cake which Miss Hannah had baked for the occasion, all washed down with glassfuls of home-made wine. Jamie was allowed to stay up later, and told me in detail of his two days without me, and how he had helped Miss Hannah with her baking, and had collected in the eggs all by himself.

I spent a long time putting him to bed that night, and singing to him, for — 'Jamie not sleep without you, Mama.' So he went to Uncle David's room and slept in his bed, much to

Miss Hannah's consternation.

Poor David, I thought, hugging the little boy to me. His bed was narrow enough without an extra wriggling little body in it as well.

I left Jamie snug and drowsy and went downstairs to find Miss Hannah already making steps to depart.

'Dearie me, Mrs Wood, the little lad fair wore me out with questions and chatter. It was Mama this, and Mama that, and when will Mama come back to Jamie? I was indeed thankful to see you safely home again, for I do not believe he would have slept another night without you.'

'He did not sleep the one night on his own,' I answered, throwing a smile at David, 'the naughty boy kept Uncle David awake for most of the time, I believe.'

'He did not disturb me, Beth, and we comforted each other. It was so strange without you, although Hannah took over magnificently.'

'Why does she call you Mrs Wood?'

asked Merry in a high, clear voice. 'And Jamie is not the right name, either. Why do you tell so many lies, Elizabeth?'

There was silence for a moment, then Miss Hannah made for the door, murmuring that she would collect her belongings ready for going home, and I sank down at the kitchen table wondering what to say, and David cleared his throat.

'Your sister made a new life with us, Miss Meredith, and decided to have a new name at the same time,' he explained. 'It is not often that one has the chance to be re-born, so to speak, but here at Starrling anything is possible. It will help you to start afresh, also, and I am so glad that Beth has brought you here. I know she will enjoy your company, and hope that you will be happy with us.'

'Thank you, Mr Starr.' She smiled radiantly at him and looked almost like her old attractive self.

'I do not know about you, Merry,' I said, 'but I should dearly love a bath.

Could we take over the kitchen, David, whilst you walk Miss Hannah home?'

'Of course.'

He brought the heavy tin bath in from the larder, where it rested for most of the time under the trestle table, and he also filled two pans with water and carried them over to the stove.

'There. I shall now leave you two ladies to your ablutions, and will come back in the front way so as not to disturb you.'

His smile at me was warm, and I knew that he was as pleased to have me back as I was to be there.

'What a considerate man!' Merry gazed after him in admiration. 'How did he hurt his leg, Elizabeth?'

I explained a little about David's past life, but was so weary by then that I could not go into details. Then I dragged myself upstairs to search for something for Merry to wear until there was time to make her new clothes. Jamie breathed gently from his cot, and when I had found a clean night-gown, and a blouse and skirt of mine which she could put on for the morning, I leaned over and dropped a light kiss on his forehead.

'Sweet dreams, my son,' I whispered, and went downstairs with jubilation in my heart. Now we were all together again and my family was complete.

The next day Merry looked a different person. I had washed her hair the night before, and with her fresh clothes and clean body, she looked more like the Merry of three years back. She was far too thin, and there was a tension about her neck and shoulders, a twitch to her mouth, which was new to me. But she assured me that she had had a comfortable night in the four-poster, and her appearance enlivened the breakfast table.

David chatted quite vigorously for him, Miriam, with her newly acquired good humour, almost sparkled, and Job could not take his eyes off my sister. He became pathetically fond of her over the next weeks, and David had to speak sharply to him, for he did not do his work properly and would stare moodily into space, or else disappear in the direction of the house where he put himself at Merry's disposal.

My first job was to see that Merry was adequately clad, and after David had been to market and brought back some pretty blue and pink cloth for us, I set her to cutting and stitching whilst I did the housework. She had always been good with her needle, and the work helped to occupy her, for she was restless despite her need for peace and quiet, and I feared that our life at Starrling would bore her.

To begin with she was busy enough, going around the yard and sheds with Jamie, picking and arranging flowers, for she had always been clever in artistic ways and I thankfully left the vases for her to do; and she sewed away at every odd moment. But all too soon her wardrobe was complete and she became impatient and querulous. What were we to do with her during the long winter months ahead?

'Can we not go into town, Elizabeth?' she asked one Monday, as I was thumping away at the wash tub. 'I should dearly love to see some shops and new faces for a change. How you put up with this dreary life, I do not know. And as for those breeches you are always wearing — I find them abominable! You should get out more, Elizabeth, for 'tis obvious this life is having an ill effect on you.' She put down her needle and began tapping her fingers on the table top. 'Can you not ask David for the horse and cart tomorrow?'

'I am afraid they are being used daily in the fields, and it is not wise to go about in public, Merry. Here we are safe and I wish to remain that way. As for my appearance, I am sorry if it offends you, but it is sensible garb for all the work I do.'

'Safe! What good is that when I am likely to die of boredom,' she exclaimed pettishly. 'Do you never entertain,

Elizabeth? Have you no friends, or visitors? And what about Jamie? He should go out and about more or he will grow up believing that the world begins and ends at Starrling.'

'Merry.' I turned away from the tub, my soapy hands going to my hips. 'Do you realise *why* we are here? I do not wish to bring the subject up as it appears to upset you, but we are all here because of *your* association with Mr Lucas Silver.'

'I know, dearest, and he was a terrible man, but he would never think to look for us here. Anyway, he is sure to have lost interest by now and he has that Arabella to console him.'

'Where was she all the time you lived on the house-boat?'

'He set her up in a nice apartment, so she told me. *She* would not deign to live on the river, but it was the only place Lucas could keep me. Locked up all day long, Elizabeth, and most nights, too.' Her face began to crumple.

'Does he still perform?' I asked quickly.

'Naturally, for he needs money. I was no longer of use to him because I was ill and my looks went and he despised me. But he cannot manage so well with that female, I know he cannot! Elizabeth, why do you make me think of him?' And she began to sob in earnest.

'Now, Merry, dry your eyes and get on with your sewing.' I was becoming tired of her tears the moment I tried to find out anything about Silver, and lacked the patience with which I used to comfort her. 'Be thankful that you are safe and sound in a good home,' I said, returning to my washing, 'and your health has greatly improved during the last weeks.'

'It has not! You do not know how ill I feel looking at you and this beastly room all day long! I shall go to bed now.' She slammed down her sewing. 'Do not call me down for lunch, for I am not hungry.' And she fled from the room.

Merry did not re-appear until evening, and then she emerged with a new ribbon in her hair, and with her face rosy and freshly washed. She was charming and gay, and chattered to David as if nothing were the matter. After dinner he taught her cribbage, whilst I patched the breeches which I had torn in the garden that afternoon.

In fact that was to be the pattern of the next weeks. Merry, irritable and weepy with me during the day, but appearing sweetly vivacious for David's benefit at night. She scorned housework and would not so much as cross the yard in bad weather, for fear of dirtying the hem of her gown; she would not help with the cooking or washing up, and kept repeating that she was bored.

Yet once David was in for the night and we sat companionably by the fireside, she would ask him questions about his day, showing an amazing interest in animal husbandry, and beg him to read aloud to her, or teach her some new card game.

She looked demure and very feminine in the dresses which she now possessed, and her hair, which she washed frequently, began to shine and curl again, and her hands remained soft, white, and useless.

It was a miraculous change from the skinny little creature whom I had collected from the Drew's house, but made me feel unattractive in my stained breeches and masculine shirts, knowing that my dark skin and work-worn hands compared unfavourably to Merry's.

Although my sister had both Job's and David's hearts, Jamie remained faithful to me and did not seem over-impressed by his pretty aunt. But I watched carefully, night after night, seeing Merry's golden curls mingling with David's fair hair as she leaned over his shoulder to read some verse or passage from a book, and I realised that she was flirting with him as she had once done with Mr Arthur. I had not cared for the mournful Mr Drew, but David Starr had once asked me to marry him and I did not intend losing him to my young sister.

Eventually, I tackled him in the pig-sty.

One Sunday the sow farrowed and as the Gritts were free after milking, David was on his own. It was very windy that day so Merry would not venture out, and I made my way hastily over to the pen in order to say my piece before he came into the house.

It was not a romantic setting, he, standing in the sty, with his hair ruffled and blood on his hands, and I standing without, my hair blowing across my face, fury in my heart.

'What is it, Beth?' David came across to the low wall which divided us. 'Anything wrong?'

'You once said you wanted to marry me. Does that offer still stand?' I spoke stiffly, hating to be so outspoken yet knowing no other way of getting a direct and instant answer.

'It does.'

'Then please marry me as soon as

possible, I have changed my mind.'

'I see.' His mouth twitched in a most unlover-like fashion, and to my surprise he looked amused. 'I shall arrange it with Parson Roberts at once. Would you like it in a week, or a month, or when?'

'We will have to wait for the banns to be called — but after that, at once.' I could not understand his amusement. 'Is it so very funny, then, the idea of marriage to me?'

David's face softened and his eyes lost their shine of merriment. 'No, Beth, I am deeply honoured by your decision; it is only the present situation which I find comical. Here we are, you and I, standing knee deep in mud and straw, both in breeches and shirt-sleeves, discussing matrimony. You must see the funny side, must you not?'

'It makes more sense than trying to speak to you in the house, with Merry's hair falling over your shoulders and her bosom falling into your face,' I answered crossly.

'Be gentle with her, Beth, for she is still unwell.'

'She is fully mended now and sleeps and eats perfectly adequately. You should not waste so much of your time on her.'

'Merry is sound in body,' he replied soberly, 'but her mind is not yet right. She is still very frightened.'

'Frightened?' I stared at him.

He nodded. 'She is like a nervous, worried animal, and needs careful handling. Be kind, Beth, for you have done so much up until now — do not let impatience spoil your natural generosity.'

'As long as you remember that *I* am to become your wife I shall do my best for her.' Sighing, I turned away from him. 'We could be such fine companions if only she would not rile me so! You are only with her for short periods and see her best side, David, but I have her with me all day long and her petulance angers me.'

'Nevertheless, go carefully. I fear it

will be some time before your sister is fully recovered from her past ordeal.'

I shrugged and squelched my way back across the yard. Doubtless David knew more about such things, living close to nature and tending sick animals, as he did. But it was surprising that he had seen through her façade, for she always put on a special show for him of an evening, which had quite fooled me.

11

We were married, David and I, on the second Saturday in October, and for the last time I reverted to my maiden name. Thus Elizabeth Allwood, spinster, and David Michael Starr, bachelor, were wed in the parish church of St Edward's by Parson Roberts.

I feared Lucas Silver no longer, and strangely, since Merry had been with us, had received no further communication from him, nor, I was sure, had Jamie. So I believed that we had rid ourselves of him for good.

That Saturday was overshadowed by no feelings of doubt or gloom, and I, a sober but satisfied bride in my best grey silk gown, took David to be my wedded husband, and felt a small glow of triumph. Miss Hannah and Merry witnessed our espousal, and Samuel Gritt gave me away in his Sunday suit, shuffling and ducking his head in embarrassment at the honour, prodded on by Miriam, with Job and Jamie grinning delightedly from the front pew. It was altogether a simple but happy family occasion.

We went back to celebrate in the warm kitchen at Starrling, and our company did not depart until after eleven o'clock that night.

Merry had taken the news very well. I had thought she might have sulked, or been annoyed when I told her, but she had kissed me and seemed genuinely pleased about our marriage. So much so that I regretted the harsh thoughts I had had about her, and vowed to myself that I would do everything within my power to make her life a happy one, even perhaps to venture into town with her in the near future.

Jamie, too, had taken it all in his stride. I had been unsure about his reaction, for my bed had been moved into David's room, and the boy would have to sleep alone for the first time in his life. But he had agreed that as he was older he should have a room of his own.

'Mama is just across the passage,' I told him, 'and you can leave your door open so I shall hear you at once if you need me.'

'Mama and Papa David,' he agreed, 'still close to Jamie. Not go to big room with Aunt Merry.'

'Oh, no, darling, we won't move there.' What ever had given him that idea?

Perhaps Merry had assumed that we would require the four-poster and thus throw her out? At the thought of the bed I went hot and hastily bundled Jamie into his bed and kissed him goodnight. Then I went thoughtfully downstairs.

I did not love David, but I felt enough affection for him to know that our marriage could be successful as long as I tried hard to care for him, and restrained my temper. He was a good, kind man; he was also intelligent, and a gentleman. I knew that both my mother and my father would have considered him a splendid match despite his lack of wealth. But the thought of sharing his bedroom made me nervous, and I wondered if it would be possible to get a little bit tipsy before we had to go upstairs together.

I joined our guests in the kitchen and made merry with them, drinking as much of my home-made wine as I decently could. But once they had all left and my sister had retired for the night, the time came for us to go to David's austere and tidy room as man and wife.

I sat at the table twiddling my fingers.

'Well, Beth, what troubles you?' My husband was standing with his back to the fire, gazing at me with tender amusement.

'Nothing.' I met his gaze squarely. 'That is, I hope you will not be disappointed in me — I shall try very hard to make you a good wife.'

'I know you will.' The amusement left David's face and he moved across to the table where I was sitting, and placed a hand upon my shoulder. 'Do not worry, Beth. We shall carry on living here exactly as we have done this past year, and I shall expect no more from you save what you have given me up until now.'

'What do you mean?' I looked up into his face and thought how tired he appeared. If only I could have given him a dowry he would have been able to employ more labourers and would not need to work so hard himself.

I had offered David a portion of the money I had in the bank from the sale of my house, but he had refused to touch it. It was mine, mine and Jamie's, he had insisted, and must remain in my possession as a safeguard for my future.

'I mean,' David said, 'that you will continue to cook and clean for me, and give me your companionship and loyalty, that is all. I know that you do not love me and this will be a marriage of convenience, Beth, until, or unless, you happen to fall in love with me.'

My heart began to beat in sharp little jerks. 'Why, David?' I wanted to make him a good wife, to repay in every way the kindness and the security which he had so generously given to Jamie and me. 'I will try and love you, I really will.'

'I know,' he answered quietly, 'but that is not enough. You see, I love you very much, and I want — indeed I expect — that same love from you. If you do not feel able to share my feelings then I would rather have nothing at all.' He took my face in his hands, caressing my cheeks with his thumbs. 'When you come to me and say that you truly love me, then, my dear one, I shall take you to my bed and we will share our passion.'

Briefly he lowered his head and his lips touched mine, and so sweet, so gentle was his kiss, that I leaned against him, wondering at my own response, amazed at the swift rush of blood which flooded my neck and face. My hands went up to his shoulders and I was about to pull him close when he lifted his head and stepped back.

'That was foolish of me.' David limped away calling to the cats, and I was left sitting, weak and empty, in the middle of the room.

'Out, out, you miserable creatures,' he said, in mock anger, holding the door wide and then moving to stir them with his foot. 'Out, you lazy monsters, and do some work!' They were all out at last and he closed and bolted the door behind them. 'Off you go, Beth, and sleep well. I'll see you in the morning at breakfast.'

David's tone was brisk and he would not meet my eyes, and for that night and for those that followed, he slept upon the hard kitchen floor covered with a blanket. Nobody else knew, for he was always the first to rise, but I felt cheated. I had meant to make him a good wife in every way and yet he would give me no chance to prove myself. However, after that first disturbing embrace, I recovered my equilibrium and accepted the fact that ours would be a marriage of convenience from then on, for in no way could I see the situation changing.

A few days after our wedding, Merry took Jamie blackberrying, or rather, Jamie took my sister, for he rushed ahead with the basket and she moved sedately behind, picking up her skirts and treading carefully for fear of cow pats and thistles.

I watched them go, then busied myself in the garden. There was much to do before winter set in, and less time now that Merry was forever at my heels, wanting to chat, or asking if she could help, and being more of a hindrance with her dislike of the soil on her hands, and the damp air which played havoc with her carefully arranged hair.

This afternoon was fine and clear and I was glad to see the two of them go off so amicably. Merry did not spend much time with the boy, and I hoped that time spent like this, on their own, might help to develop a friendship which was curiously tepid on both sides.

I worked hard all afternoon, then went in to wash and prepare tea, knowing that their outing would have made the two of them hungry. David arrived back, but there was no sign of Merry or my son and I began to worry.

'Do not fret,' said David, 'they probably wandered further than they realised.'

But as the day began to darken and we had waited for more than an hour, we both knew that something was wrong.

'Stay here,' David said, and calling for Jip he made for the door.

At that moment Merry appeared in the yard, a basket over her arm, but no small boy plodding at her side.

I ran past David and flew at her. 'Where is he? Where's Jamie?' I shouted, grasping her by one thin shoulder. 'What have you done with him?'

'Jamie?' She lifted vacant eyes to my face and I saw with horror that she had a silly, half-smile on her slack lips. 'Jamie gone — Barnaby gone — all gone.' And she giggled inanely.

David pushed between us and shoved me away as I made to strike her. 'Beth — stop!' he cried sharply. 'Can you not see that she is demented? Come in, Merry, love, and warm yourself.' He helped her into the lighted kitchen and sat her down and began rubbing her hands. 'You brought some beautiful blackberries,' he said gently, 'that was clever of you. Did you go far, Merry?'

'Far, far,' she repeated, in a high piping voice. 'Far away and no one will find him.'

'Merry, where is Jamie?' I bent forward and spoke urgently into her stupid blank face. 'Where is my son? Where did you leave him?'

'Safe, quite safe. Lucas won't find

259

him now. No one will find him now.'
And she patted David's head as he
knelt before her.

I strode to the door, flinging on an
old coat which hung behind it.

'Beth, wait!' called David, but I was
out, running across the yard, making
for the gate in the hedge through which
I had last seen them pass so many
hours ago — too many hours ago. Jamie
had only been wearing a thin shirt and
it had now grown chill, and the air was
damp.

'Jamie!' I shouted at the top of my
voice. 'Jamie, where are you?'

But there was silence and no little
voice called cheerily back.

I plodded down one field following
the hedge, searching frantically in my
mind for the position of the best
blackberry bushes. Where had I gone
previously with Jamie? In which direction would they most likely have gone?
It was really dark now, and I had left in
such haste that I had forgotten the
lantern. My shoes slipped and slithered

in the mud, and brambles tore at my breeches; I had not stopped to put on my heavy boots and the going was difficult in the darkness.

Suddenly, without thinking, I began to call Jamie in my mind, saying his name over and over again. He had never answered me before, always coming bodily to me, usually at a run. But possibly, if I called loud and long enough, he would answer even if he could not move towards me.

JAMIE, JAMIE, WHERE ARE YOU, DARLING?

And faintly, so softly that I could not be sure at first, I heard an answering call.

MAMA!

I stood quite still, concentrating with all my might.

JAMIE, WHERE ARE YOU? TELL MAMA WHERE YOU ARE. ARE YOU IN A FIELD? OR NEAR THE CHURCH? WHERE, DARLING, WHERE?

MAMA, COME QUICK.

WHERE, JAMIE?

IN THE WOOD — BY THE BIG TREES.

I knew that! At the furthest end of the farm, through three more fields and down the slope at the bottom was the wood, which bordered the farm down one side. Fortunately, the moon appeared at that moment sliding through a bank of cloud to shine clear and white upon the land. Taking advantage of the brightness I ran, ran as I had never run before, across one field, over the gate, no time to stop and open it, across another field, through a gap in the hedge, and then I was in the last meadow with the grass sloping away from me down to the blackness of the wood.

I'M COMING, JAMIE. WAIT FOR MAMA. ARE YOU ALL RIGHT?

And back came the small voice,

JAMIE HERE — COME QUICK, MAMA. JAMIE FRIGHTENED.

In the wood it was very quiet and frighteningly eerie, with the trunks tall

262

and awesome all around, and the strange rustling sounds of leaves and little night animals. I found a path and followed it thankfully, believing that my sister would not have strayed far into the undergrowth.

'Jamie,' I called out aloud, 'Jamie, where are you?'

And in a narrow ditch beside the path, I found my son crouched, half-covered with leaves and branches. He was shivering and very cold, but he was alive and I gathered him up into my arms, warming his trembling body with the folds of my coat, pressing him to me in agonised relief.

'Dear love, thank God you are safe! Mama is here now and all is well, Jamie. I've come to take you home.'

'Aunt Merry say stay here.' His teeth were chattering, and his voice was hoarse. 'Not move, she say. Jamie not like it, Mama, so cold and dark.' He spoke quickly, clutching me tightly around the neck, his little fists like ice against my skin. 'Jamie want Mama but

Aunt Merry say no, no! Big man get Jamie. Jamie stay.'

He began to cry, thrusting his face into my hair, his body racked by sobs.

'Don't worry about anything, my love.' I was walking back up the path, dreading the long trail home yet finding strength to hurry despite my fatigue. 'Mama will take you home and give you a nice hot bath, and we'll have a cup of tea by the fire. Then you can sleep in Mama's bed tonight, Jamie? How about that? Isn't that a fine idea?'

I talked on, not knowing what I was saying, seeking to comfort the child with the sound of my voice. Gradually his shivering stopped and he drew warmth from my body as I laboured back up the rise, blundering across the fields, my shoes solid with mud and the boy becoming heavier in my arms with every step. But the pain did not matter, nor the weariness. For I had my son safely back with me, and joy filled my heart, mixed with intense anger at Merry.

In the last field I heard a dog barking, then Jip's low form bounded out of the darkness and far behind I saw the faint glow of a lantern.

'Beth!' David called, but I had no strength to reply and sank down upon the wet grass, too exhausted to move another step. Jip's barking brought David to us, and he exclaimed in shock as he saw me huddled upon the ground, the boy's body in my arms.

'Beth, is he all right? What has happened to him? Where did you find him?'

He helped me to my feet and made to take Jamie from me.

'No,' I said hoarsely, scarcely able to speak, 'do not touch him. Take my arm and help me to get home.'

With David supporting my right arm, taking much of the weight from off my trembling legs, we staggered on and finally reached the house.

'Hannah is upstairs with Merry,' David said, pulling out a chair for me. 'I had to go down and fetch her as I did not dare leave your sister alone.'

'In that time this child could have caught his death of cold.' I stared grimly up at him. 'Put water on for a bath and get us some tea quickly. Then go up and fetch his night clothes.'

My tone was rude but I had to hurt somebody, had to vent the wrath which was burning within my bosom, and David was near whereas Merry was not.

My husband obeyed my commands without speaking, but as he passed the chair where I sat rocking the tired child, he put out his hand and stroked Jamie's curly head.

'It's good to have you back again, my son. Tell me all about your adventures tomorrow.'

Jamie smiled sleepily. 'Night, Papa David,' he murmured, and snuggled closer to my chest.

That night, after David returned from taking Miss Hannah home, and I sat drinking cup after cup of hot, sweet tea, which was all I could stomach, he informed me that he would sleep outside Merry's room that night.

'Why not in it?' I retorted. 'No doubt that is what she has always wanted.'

'Your sister's mind is greatly muddled and I fear for her sanity. She must not be left alone for a while.'

'Then she should see a doctor, or be put away,' I said.

'Hannah brought some powders with her and has given Meredith a sleeping draught. I do beg you not to mention anything about this escapade tomorrow, Beth. She must forget the whole mad affair and we must help her by behaving normally.

'I cannot,' I said stonily. 'What of Jamie's state of mind? How can he behave as if nothing has happened? You worry about my sister's mind, but I am fearful for my son's *life*!'

'Children have marvellous powers of recuperation, and Jamie is very secure in the knowledge of your love, and mine, Beth. You must tell him that Meredith was playing a game of hide and seek and that you were sent to find him. I believe that he will accept that explanation readily enough in the morning once he is rested.'

I snorted. 'Any excuse will do to cover up Merry's crime!'

'She meant the boy no harm, Beth. She kept insisting that he was safe. I can tell that her fear is of Lucas Silver, and she wishes to conceal the boy from him. She would never hurt Jamie, of that I am sure.'

'I am not.' I stood up, rubbing my aching back. 'Jamie sleeps with me tonight and you may put your body where you will. But this I tell you, Merry is never to be left alone with my son again — never! Is that understood?'

'If you say so. But you, in turn, must guard your tongue. I cannot forbid you to remain alone with your sister, but I can ask you to be prudent. I think that she, too, will remember little of this day's events — '

'Crime!'

'Events,' he repeated firmly, 'but can only become better and recover her health if you co-operate.'

'I shall do my best.' I walked to the door and opened it. 'But I have an ominous feeling that Merry's presence here is going to ruin all our lives.'

Let him get out his Bible and pray about that, I thought, and marched upstairs to join my son who was sleeping peacefully in my bed.

12

On the twelfth day of November dear Miss Hannah died. She went peacefully in her sleep, and David found her in the afternoon when he took the cart down with a load of logs for her fire.

He was terribly upset for she was the only 'family' he had left, and she had always been a loving and loyal friend. I was also greatly saddened by the loss, and knew that Starrling would never be quite the same without the kindly, cheerful woman on whom we had all depended so much.

I sent a hurried note to my Miss Bloster, informing her about the funeral, and with mixed feelings, for it should have been a joyful reunion, we greeted each other, after she had come driving over in a hired carriage.

There were few mourners for Hannah, like us, had led a secluded existence, Starrling and David's faithful attendance being all that she required from life.

Samuel and Job Gritt went, and David and Miss Bloster were chief mourners. I did not wish to attend for fear of leaving Jamie, but David arranged for Miriam to spend the afternoon in the house with Merry and the boy, and I impressed upon her that she must remain with Jamie for the entire time that we were away.

My sister had improved greatly since her breakdown, and appeared her normal, frivolous self, but I did not trust her, and only attended the funeral because I knew that Miriam was up at the house, and because I had had a deep affection for Miss Hannah and wished to accompany her on her last journey to the little plot beside the church.

We walked over the fields, Miss Bloster, David and I, for it was quicker than going round by the road, and there was a footpath to the church which was not yet too muddied by rain.

The Gritts and two men from the village who were acting as pallbearers, met us in the porch, and the service was mercifully short. My heart was full as I was reminded of Father's going, and all the many worries and troubles which had beset me since his passing.

My thoughts were rudely shattered, however, as we emerged into the churchyard, out into the pale sunlight of that terrifying afternoon. For running down the path and throwing herself at the lych-gate was Miriam, her hair in wild disorder, her hands raised and jerking before her.

'Master David, Master David, come quickly! Oh, Madam, forgive me,' she jabbered, rushing past the bearers and the affronted Parson, leaping at me with feverish eyes. 'I was in the privy but for a moment, and Miss Merry wedged the door from the outside so that I could not open it, and Madam, she and the boy are gone and so is the carriage.'

'What?' cried David, rounding on her and taking her by the arm. 'Where have they gone?'

But I did not wait for words. Picking up my skirts I ran, through the gate and across the fields, my bonnet flying from off my head, losing one shoe on the path behind me.

I knew, knew at once where Merry had gone. She was taking Jamie back to Lucifer. Seeing Miss Bloster's waiting carriage, and no doubt bribing the bored driver, she had ordered him to drive her into town and thence to the railway station.

All her talk about escaping from Lucas Silver had been nonsense — that was clear to me now. He had allowed her to go, hoping that I would believe her miserable story and thus take her into my home, which would enable her to seek out Jamie and eventually abduct him.

How they had got away from Miriam I cared not; all I wanted was the horse and cart, in a frantic effort to overtake them, to stop them from boarding the London train.

My hands were trembling so violently that I could not harness Caesar, so I threw the rope halter around his neck, hurled myself up on to his broad back, and rode him as I was, petticoats and shawl awry, bonnet dangling by its ribbons down my back, rode him down the drive and out on to the road in the direction of town.

It was situated five miles east of our village, and the lumbering old horse had not a hope of catching the spry bay which had pulled Miss Bloster's light vehicle. But so maddened was I by rage and grief, that I could not think clearly and beat at Caesar with the rope end of the halter, thumping the brute with my heels and fists, shrieking at him to go faster.

As we clattered towards the village, David came at a run from the side road which led up to the church, and flung himself at the horse, dragging it to a standstill.

'Beth, get down!' he shouted.

'Let go, let go of him! I will ride further — I will kill her for this!'

'You cannot hope to catch up with them on Caesar. Get down and discuss this calmly. You are in no fit state to ride.'

'I am, damn you, let go!' And I lifted the end of the rope and struck at his face in fury.

A red weal appeared across his cheek, and he caught the rope and wrenched it from my grasp, then his hand clamped down upon my leg and he tugged me from the horse, spilling me roughly into the road.

'David!' I screamed, scrambling to my feet, hitting out at him with clenched fists. 'They will get away! She has taken my baby and I'll never see him again!'

I burst into a storm of weeping and he folded me against him, holding my struggling body close, talking sooth-ingly, trying to calm me.

'We will follow, Beth, trust me and

we will find Jamie. But you need money, my dear, and luggage. Use your head and listen to me.'

David rocked me in his arms until my sobs died down and he could make himself heard.

'Tomorrow we will go to London, Beth, I shall accompany you and we will find the boy. Now let us go home and make plans in peace and quiet.'

As he was speaking there was the sound of hooves behind us and Miss Bloster's hired carriage drove into sight. David let go of me and I leaned weakly against Caesar's sweating neck, as he hailed the driver. I did not hear what was said for my mind was filled with thoughts of Jamie, and the terrible knowledge that Lucifer would soon possess him. Once that happened my son would be lost to me forever.

Then David took my arm and helped me into the carriage, and after tying Caesar to the rear and telling the driver to go slowly, he climbed in beside me and held me close all the way back to Starrling.

I did not speak; there was nothing to say. But David took over completely, and fed everyone and saw Miss Bloster away after tea. He reassured Miriam, who kept staring at me and trying to explain, but I turned my face to the wall and her miserable excuses fell on deaf ears. He arranged with Samuel about the following day, for Samuel was to be in charge of the farm during our absence.

I sat beside the hearth, uncaring, my eyes seeing Jamie's face, my arms aching for his sturdy little body.

David undressed me and put me to bed, and that night he lay beside me, holding me in his arms. But his presence was meaningless, and his words meant nothing, for there was only one course for me to take and I knew with awful certainty what I must do.

I did not call Jamie, either that night or in the morning, it would only have upset him and there was no way in which he could come to me. But I sent out loving thoughts, warm and strong, telling him that I was coming, and not to be afraid. It was all I could do, as David packed a bag for us and made me eat some porridge which he spooned into my mouth. He talked and explained, kind David, what we would do in London, where we would stay, and what enquiries he would make. I followed docilely when he led the way to the stables, and Samuel came with us into town in order to drive the cart back afterwards.

The train journey made no impression on me, and London seemed noisy and over-crowded, a dismal blur that grey November day. I took in little of my surroundings and was ensconced in a small, alien hotel before I was fully aware of it.

'Where are we?' I asked, as David unpacked our few belongings and turned back the bed covers.

'In an hotel in Sloane Street,' he

answered gently, helping me off with my cloak and hat, sitting me upon the bed and removing my shoes. 'I have ordered a hot drink for you, Beth, so drink it and then try and get some sleep. I am going out at once to start enquiries and will be back soon with good news, I am sure. So stay here, my love, and rest awhile.'

I nodded and laid myself obediently upon the bed, and sipped at the hot milk when it came. But the moment David had left the room I dressed myself, and took off my cross and chain, which I left carefully upon the bed. Then I went out, shutting the door behind me.

Silver's houseboat was at Chelsea, and I was certain that he would be there; if not, I would wait until he did turn up. Now that he had my sister and my child, he could have me, also. There was no more fight left in me. Even the hatred which I had felt for Merry had now vanished.

If I should find Jamie and manage to

escape with him — what hope was there for a serene future? Lucas Silver would always hunt us, with Merry's help or without it, and we would live in continual fear. I could run and hide no longer — in the end Lucifer had won.

My decision would be hard on David, who had grown fond of me and Jamie; but our marriage was a union in name only and had never been consummated. What he had never possessed he could not miss too greatly, and as he had managed quite well with his life before knowing me, it was certain that he would survive as he had done before. There was little doubt that his life would be more tranquil without my presence.

After enquiring the way to the river from the clerk at the desk, I found my way through narrow back streets, my cloak wrapped around my body, a shawl covering my hair, and walked swiftly in the direction of Chelsea. After stopping once for further instructions, I did not pause again and made my way unmolested down to the embankment.

Silver's boat was the last but one in the row and it was a strange walk, traversing one boat after another, for they were planked together and I had to cross many different homes before reaching the one I wanted.

The water shone like black oil, reflecting the lamps in the street, and the smells and sounds were different to those of the countryside; sudden bursts of raucous laughter sounded from behind tiny lighted windows, an accordion played somewhere within, accompanied by rough singing, a thin cat spat at me and fled, whilst people cooked and banged and shouted in their cramped quarters as I stumbled by.

Silver's boat was ominously silent, with no child's voice raised in fright or anger; no sound of music either, or even of voices. But a light shone through one curtained window so that I knew somebody was there. A little breeze sprung up as I hesitated, filling my nostrils with the unpleasant tang of dirty river water, polluting rubbish and greasy food.

I put my hand on the door and opened it without knocking.

Inside the air was warm and stale, and an oil lamp at one end of the low room lit but a quarter of the space. Piles of books rested on the table in the middle, and at the far end of it sat Lucas Silver, his head bent, reading.

Cages swung across one wall, half in darkness, filled with huddled shapes, and there was a mess of corn and chaff and bird droppings upon the wooden floor. The flickering of the lamp must have given away my entry, for as I shut the door noiselessly behind me, Silver raised his head.

'So,' he said, 'you have come, Elizabeth. I was expecting you.'

'Where is Jamie?'

His bearded face appeared thinner, but otherwise he looked exactly as I had last seen him, the same vile medallion about his neck, the same black robes upon his frame.

'Jamie? Ah, you mean Barnaby. He is safe.' His eyes caught the light, glinting, as he watched me.

'Is he *here*, Mr Silver?'

He nodded gravely. 'The boy is in the back, asleep with his mother.'

His mother! That half-demented, scheming creature was nothing more than a pawn of Lucifer's, she was not Jamie's mother, I was. But I swallowed the quick retort which sprang to my lips and took a deep breath.

'You have taken my sister away from me, and now you possess my son. You might as well have me also, Lucas Silver, for I cannot live without Jamie.'

'Why should I take you in? You have caused me great trouble, Elizabeth, and made me angry. No one has ever defied me before but you did so. And, what is more, you dared to use your powers against me.' He stood up and moved round the table towards me, his shadow flung huge and menacing against the wall. 'You dared to fight me and you almost won. Do you realise that?'

'I would have won if it had not been for Merry's treachery.'

He nodded. 'I could no longer get through to you, or to the boy. You had set up some obstacle in my way — what was it, Elizabeth? How did you withstand me?'

With a Bible, I thought dully, and with the love of a good man.

But that was behind me. Starrling and David must fade into the background until they became but distant memories. I belonged to their world no longer. My future was here, with the man who had disrupted my life four years ago and who would not be repulsed.

I lifted my chin. 'I am here, Lucas Silver. Do with me what you will. I will do anything for you, or with you, as long as you allow me to stay with Jamie. I cannot give him up.'

'Such love!' His teeth showed for a moment in the thick forest of his beard.

'What must I do to earn such devotion? How can I inspire such single-minded purpose? For I will have you, Elizabeth, body and soul, as once I promised.'

'I am here.'

'In body, yes, but not yet in spirit. Oh, you are low, depressed, weary, I can see that. But you are not yet beaten, Elizabeth, and I will stand no more defiance. Do you understand?'

I looked up at him and our eyes met and locked in battle.

I would not give in to him — ever. He could take my body, but my mind would remain separate, acting and thinking for me. Never would he take over my thoughts and govern my spirit as he manipulated Merry's.

'I see.' Silver's gaze dropped away from my face and his hand went up to toy with the medallion upon his breast.

Seeing his movement I caught my bottom lip between my teeth, panic rising within my bosom. I knew what was passing through his mind and I was suddenly afraid.

'Not that,' I said.

Not the snake, not that foul, writhing reptile again. I could not bear it. My limbs began to tremble as I groped for the back of a chair which was set against the table, horror beginning to lick through my stomach as my stubborn pride started to melt. I could stand up to Lucifer, had believed that I need fear him no longer, but he still possessed this one weapon against which I was defenceless.

As I stood holding on to the chair, sickened in mind and body, the door at the far end of the room opened and I glimpsed Merry slipping through, to stand with her back to the door, her face a pale blur in the shadows.

Desperation gave me a moment's courage.

'I will love you, Lucas Silver,' I said clearly, 'and I promise to stay by you and not attempt to take Jamie away. I will care for you, cook for you, work for you and love you. Is that not enough?'

'From you? No. I desire more than

that. Your body I can take, that is simple. And I should expect care and attention. Yes, and loyalty. But I want your mind, also, Elizabeth. It is too strong a force to be working constantly against me — I cannot be forever on my guard, and you would, with cunning and patience, scheme against me. That, you must understand, would be intolerable.'

As he was speaking, Merry moved behind him towards the sideboard where the remains of a meal stood uncovered. From the corner of my eye I saw her pick up a long sharp bread knife.

'Perhaps,' I said quickly, keeping my eyes steady on his face, 'perhaps, if I could make my mind go blank you could hypnotise me as you did once at home, the day you gave Jamie the bean necklace. Then there would be no need of the snake, Mr Silver. Look at me now and try — I shall not fight you.' I spoke carefully, willing him to concentrate on me so that he did not notice what was going on in the shadows behind him. 'I could bear anything except that reptile again, so try, I beg you, for there is no strength left in me and I have had enough this day.'

Silver looked at me then and I tried to go blank, tried to shut out the picture of Merry creeping up on him, her arm raised and the evil blade catching the light as she struck.

But he must have seen something in my expression, guessed at danger, for he turned even as Merry attacked, and caught the blow full upon his chest. His robes were thick but the knife was sharp, and she was striking again and again with maniacal strength, as I rushed past them to the door at the back of the room.

Slamming it behind me I saw with relief that there was a bolt, and as I rammed it to, Merry began to scream, and she screamed so loudly and with such anguish that I put my hands to my ears, terrified by the appalling noise.

There were shouts from without, the

sound of heavy boots drumming on wood, and then the houseboat began to sway as people clambered aboard.

I turned, dropping my hands, and ran to the bunk where a small figure lay.

'Jamie, are you awake? Mama is here.'

Two arms came out from beneath the ragged blankets and fastened round my neck. 'Mama,' he whispered, 'come to Jamie, Jamie frightened.'

I held him tightly, rocking his body against mine, whispering and stroking and comforting as the din went on next door.

Epilogue

It is over. All the sadness has passed, as have the fears and the nagging worries. I am home with my family, and Lucifer can harm us no longer.

We are quite a little community here now and Starrling, like the bird of that name, is beginning to look sleek and trim again, as if it is preening its feathers. Of course there is a great deal still to be done, but with money in the bank all things are possible as long as one is patient.

Merry is with us again after a long wait. They would not let us have her at first, but Cousin Grace knew some influential people, and David wrote many letters and made many journeys up to London, and now he has vouched for her security and she is home again.

My little sister, in truth, with her empty tinkling laugh and unseeing eyes.

But she is happy in her own shadowed world, and is heart-breakingly docile for most of the time. She is never left alone, and we have hired a nice young girl from the village, who lives with us and is Merry's constant companion.

At night Merry must be locked in her room, which now has ugly bars across the windows, but on her good days she goes for walks with Dora, and likes to sit in the kitchen on the stool which she carries about with her, and she watches me work, a smile upon her lips.

Job is marvellous with her; in fact she appears to converse with him, babbling away in her high childish voice, whilst he grunts and mutters back as if they are really communicating.

On Sunday afternoons, if Merry has had a reasonable day, Job calls for her at three o'clock, dressed in his best suit, with his hair smoothed down upon his low forehead, and they go down to the Lodge where Samuel and Miriam entertain her. Miriam is kind to have her, but she still feels guilty about allowing Merry to escape with Jamie, and this is her way of paying that debt. It also frees Dora who goes home on a Sunday to visit her family.

It is not a particularly pleasant life for the young girl, having to cope with Merry's many different moods, but we pay her well and she has an affection for my sister which gladdens me; I could not allow anyone to care for Merry who was harsh, or impatient. Heaven knows, Merry has had little enough happiness in her life.

But Dora knows her well, and if she tells me that my sister is having a bad day, they do not come downstairs at all, but remain cloistered above until Merry is able to face the world again.

It is also best if the children only see their aunt on her good days, and indeed, they accept her strangeness and appear fond of her.

Susie has not been with us for long. David had terrible difficulty trying to trace her, but once again, a friend of Cousin Grace's was useful in contacting the various orphanages and institutions, and they tracked her down at last, little orphaned Susie Silver, whose mother I met so long ago and was unable to help.

A poor, white-faced little baggage, Susie was, too; dirty and neglected and foul-mouthed, hating everybody and everything, and as scratchy and evil-tempered as a wild kitten. But Jamie helped her as Job helped Merry, and within weeks Susie was scampering and laughing around the fields and sheds as if she had never known any other kind of life.

David remains Papa David to both children, but I am Mama, and the sound is sweet to my ears, for at first I dared not hope that she would ever call me that.

Cousin Grace visits on occasion. Miraculously she is over her ill-health, which makes me think that Lucas Silver did have a hand in her feverish condition. She confided in me that her will had been made out in his favour up until the time that she discovered that he and Merry were lovers.

'I was a foolish old woman, Elizabeth,' she explained, 'and so lonely after Cedric's death that I allowed my heart to be taken by that wretched man. But he had a way with him, dear, and cast a spell over me for a while.'

She, it was, who directed David to the houseboat that night in London so many months ago. It was fortunate she did, for Jamie and I lay huddled on that filthy bunk for hours, breathing in the dank, foetid air, not knowing what was going on outside and too fearful to investigate. But David came, and when I heard his voice I unlocked the door, knowing that we would be safe in his company.

Lucifer's body had disappeared, and they had taken Merry away, but the smell of blood and terror remained, and I was almost fainting as David thrust his way through the inquisitive crowd and took us back to the hotel.

I was questioned by the police and had to give an account of what had happened, but the case was never brought to court because of Merry's insanity. She was shut away in an asylum for several months and David would not allow me to see her, so wild and demented was she. But he went, visiting regularly with his Bible, and gradually her frantic ravings stopped and she became calmer. It was at this stage that he applied for permission to look after her, and as the place was grossly over-crowded, and he was prepared to take full responsibility, she was finally allowed to join us here.

Why she did it, we will never know. It might have been that she was jealous because Silver desired me, whilst no longer wanting her. Or it might have been solely that she needed release from his power over her, and whilst I had his attention, her poor tortured mind grasped the opportunity to attack him whilst he was unaware.

I knew that I, too, had been to blame

for the murder, was as guilty as my sister although no weapon had been in my hand; for I had seen her actions, had known what she intended, yet had remained silent. I had wanted her to kill.

Cousin Grace also blames herself for the tragedy, and owns that but for her stupidity Merry would never have become involved with Lucas Silver, nor would we have become so embroiled in his affairs.

But she is rapidly making amends and, having taken a fancy to David, has now made out her will in his favour and has already given us more than a fair share of her wealth. At first my husband would not accept her presents, but when he realised how much our cousin could help his beloved Starrling, and when she announced that she would like a country holiday from time to time, provided it was comfortable, he gave in and has continued to accept all that she so generously gives.

David can now employ more labourers on the farm, and has been able to build new homes for them. The Gritts were given the choice of a new cottage, or of moving into Miss Hannah's old abode, and I was glad when they chose the latter.

The Lodge windows are polished and shiny now, the chimney smokes cheerily as one enters the drive, and the front garden is neat and well-stocked, for Miriam is a proud housekeeper and need work on the land no longer now that Samuel and Job receive better wages.

Miss Bloster also visits regularly in the school holidays, though not at the same time as Cousin Grace, for they do not get on. I drive over and collect her, accompanied by Jamie and Susie, and it is a very quick journey with our sprightly Nero, who shares the stall with Caesar, and our new carriage.

I glory in my role as housewife and mother, and take a full part in village life, visiting the poor and sick, and even attending church with David on Sunday mornings. The children come with us and are being brought up in a righteous manner, even if their mother has a gypsy look about her, and a strange expression in her eyes when she is angry. But I do not lose my temper often these days, and David says that he misses the devil in me.

But he does not really mean that, for I know that I make him happy, and no woman could have a better man than him. My David, whom I truly love in a way I would never have thought possible a while back.

With Lucifer's death a weight lifted from my heart, and I was able to see my husband with clearer eyes. Now we are expecting our first baby and we do not care if it is a boy or girl, for we are blessed with both a son and daughter already.

Starrling is big enough to house a large family and we hope for more children in the years to come, to fill the rooms with life and laughter, and to fully erase the grim memories of the past.

THE END

We do hope that you have enjoyed reading this large print book.

Did you know that all of our titles are available for purchase?

We publish a wide range of high quality large print books including:
Romances, Mysteries, Classics
General Fiction
Non Fiction and Westerns

Special interest titles available in large print are:
The Little Oxford Dictionary
Music Book, Song Book
Hymn Book, Service Book

Also available from us courtesy of Oxford University Press:
Young Readers' Dictionary
(large print edition)
Young Readers' Thesaurus
(large print edition)

For further information or a free brochure, please contact us at:
Ulverscroft Large Print Books Ltd.,
The Green, Bradgate Road, Anstey,
Leicester, LE7 7FU, England.
Tel: (00 44) **0116 236 4325**
Fax: (00 44) **0116 234 0205**

TOO MANY LOVES

Juliet Gray

Justin Caldwell, a famous personality of stage and screen, was blessed with good looks and charm that few women could resist. Stacy was a newcomer to England and she was not impressed by the handsome stranger; she thought him arrogant, ill-mannered and detestable. By the time that Justin desired to begin again on a new footing it was much too late to redeem himself in her eyes, for there had been too many loves in his life.

MYSTERY AT MELBECK

Gillian Kaye

Meg Bowering goes to Melbeck House in the Yorkshire Dales to nurse the rich, elderly Mrs Peacock. She likes her patient and is immediately attracted to Mrs Peacock's nephew and heir, Geoffrey, who farms nearby. But Geoffrey is a gambling man and Meg could never have foreseen the dreadful chain of events which follow. Throughout her ordeal, she is helped by the local vicar, Andrew Sheratt, and she soon discovers where her heart really lies.

HEART UNDER SIEGE

Joy St Clair

Gemma had no interest in men — which was how she had acquired the job of companion/secretary to Mrs Prescott in Kentucky. The old lady had stipulated that she wanted someone who would not want to rush off and get married. But why was the infuriating Shade Lambert so sceptical about it? Gemma was determined to prove to him that she meant what she said about remaining single — but all she proved was that she was far from immune to his devastating attraction!